NELSON ENTERTAINMENT PRESENTS AN INTERSCOPE COMMUNICATIONS PRODUCTION

BILL & TED'S BOGUS JOURNEY

KEANU REEVES   ALEX WINTER

WILLIAM SADLER   JOSS ACKLAND AND GEORGE CARLIN AS "RUFUS"

MUSIC BY DAVID NEWMAN   DIRECTOR OF PHOTOGRAPHY OLIVER WOOD   FILM EDITOR DAVID FINFER   PRODUCTION DESIGNER DAVID L. SNYDER

CO-EXECUTIVE PRODUCER NEIL MACHLIS   EXECUTIVE PRODUCERS TED FIELD AND ROBERT W. CORT

PRODUCED BY SCOTT KROOPF   WRITTEN BY CHRIS MATHESON & ED SOLOMON

BASED ON CHARACTERS CREATED BY CHRIS MATHESON & ED SOLOMON   DIRECTED BY PETER HEWITT

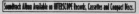 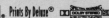

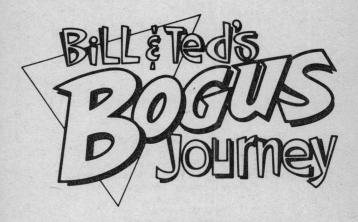

A novel by ROBERT TINE
Based on a screenplay by
CHRIS MATHESON & ED SOLOMON

B
BERKLEY BOOKS, NEW YORK

BILL & TED'S BOGUS JOURNEY

A Berkley Book / published by arrangement with
Nelson Films, Inc., Orion Pictures Corporation and
Creative Licensing Corporation

PRINTING HISTORY
Berkley edition / August 1991

ISBN: 0-425-13099-1

A BERKLEY BOOK® TM 757,375
Berkley Books are published by The Berkley Publishing
Group, 200 Madison Avenue, New York, New York 10016.
The name "BERKLEY" and the "B" logo
are trademarks belonging to Berkley Publishing Corporation.

PRINTED IN THE UNITED STATES OF AMERICA

10 9 8 7 6 5 4 3 2

A Short Introduction to the Excellent Adventures of Bill S. Preston, Esquire, and Ted "Theodore" Logan (So Far)

Being excellent to one another and partying on is not as simple as it looks. It involves a lot of hard work, time travel, a most triumphant band called Wyld Stallyns and, of course, Bill S. Preston, Esquire, and Ted "Theodore" Logan.

Not long ago Bill and Ted were more or less ordinary guys in San Dimas, a more or less ordinary town in California, and at that time, Bill and Ted had two major problems: They were flunking History and they were experiencing a total lack of babes.

Passing History was important, they thought, because if they didn't, they would totally flunk out of school (heinous) and Ted would get sent to military school in Alaska (bogus *and* heinous). It turns out, though, that was the least of their

1

problems—'cause a totally non-heinous dude called Rufus showed up from the future and informed them that the entire future of the world rested on Bill and Ted getting an A + on their History report.

So: With some assistance from the Circuits of Time, Billy the Kid, a Greek dude called Socrates, Napoleon, Ludwig van Beethoven, Joan of Arc, Genghis Khan, Abraham Lincoln and Sigmund Freud, Bill and Ted traveled back in time, then forward, met themselves in the future, set things up so they would be able to pass their History test in the past, traveled back in time, passed the test, met two totally bodacious babes, Joanna and Elizabeth, saved the world, founded their triumphant band Wyld Stallyns and decided to learn how to play the guitar.

Got it? Make sense? Excellent!

**San Dimas, California
A.D. 2691**

Chapter
1

The future is a foreign country. They do things totally triumphantly there.

By the time A.D. 2691 rolls around things will be different. The air will be clean, people will be happy, bowling scores will be way up, miniature golf scores will be way down. Things will be totally non-heinous. And who do future generations have to thank for this? Bill and Ted.

Except, don't you know it, some people are never satisfied. Take, for example, a totally bogus dude named De Nomolos. The fact that things were going bodaciously in the twenty-fifth century really bothered the guy, and he had a plan to change everything for everybody. Everything would be worse for everyone,

5

except for De Nomolos, of course. A big part of De Nomolos's plan, you see, was that he, De Nomolos, would totally rule the world. Bogus, right?

So, once again, it was up to Bill and Ted. This time they could not fail.

"It is time," said De Nomolos. His words were hard, cool, serious, like the man himself. He was seated in a dark, barren room, lit by a single shaft of light, which streamed through a single, small window high up on one bare wall.

"It is time. They have reached the second crucial turning point in their destiny. Their," he paused, and his beady eyes narrowed in disgust, "their 'message' is about to reach millions." His expression changed slowly, from one of loathing to a kind of evil happiness and pride. "We will change that."

De Nomolos was not alone in his hideaway. With him were a dozen or more students, handpicked to help him in his mission to achieve world domination. They were grim-faced, hard-looking young men and women, dressed, like their leader, from head to toe in black. All were armed. The students nodded in agreement with De Nomolos's bitter words.

"When our mission is successful, no longer will our world be dominated by the legacy of the two," his sneer intensified, "fools."

De Nomolos's followers knew when and how to get on the good side of their boss. "Idiots," they said, "morons, cretins . . ."

"And no longer," De Nomolos continued, "will we hear this hated sound . . ." His hands clawed the air in front of his chest, and the strains of a tortured air guitar split the room.

"We will stop them now," he growled. He looked at the rebels, reading determination on every face. "Are we ready?"

The rebels answered emphatically. They slammed rounds of ammunition into the chambers of their weapons and nodded.

"Onward," ordered De Nomolos.

Over at the Bill and Ted University (established A.D. 2425) it was nine o'clock in the morning and the first class air-guitar bell had just sounded. Students were assembling in a learning center—they used to be called classrooms—for their class in the Physics of Acoustical Reverberation (guitar).

No one paid much attention when the room began to vibrate, slowly at first, then faster, followed by a rush of noise, like a jet fighter taking to the skies. Then there was a shower of sparks and light exploding like a hundred rockets. When the smoke had cleared, a phone booth stood in the middle of the room. Out stepped Rufus.

Rufus was a totally triumphant dude, even for a teacher, and was well known as an old friend, mentor and advisor to Bill and Ted. Rufus, it was agreed around Bill and Ted U, was the personification of everything that is, has been or will be, rock and roll. Cool, cavalier and cocky, he dressed like a rock star and was almost never seen without his ultra-hip shades.

"Greetings, my excellent pupils. Today we continue our study of the physics of acoustical reverberation. Please meet our most non-heinous guest lecturers for the day . . ." Rufus gestured toward the phone booth and an old dude stepped out. He was gray-haired and wore a funny, old-fashioned suit, sort of like the one the fried chicken dude, Colonel Sanders, wears, only black instead of white. He bowed politely to the class.

"Say hello to our old friend, Thomas Edison, the inventor of something that used to be called the phonograph . . . that was before CDs, and you know how old *they* are. Okay. To help us out on the musical side of things, Mr. Johann Sebastian Bach." A short, fat man dressed in knee breeches and wearing a powdered wig stepped from the booth. He looked a little bewildered but managed to say, *"Guten tag, klasse . . ."*

Next up from the booth was another fine musician. "And say hello," said Rufus, "to Sir James Martin of Faith No More, founder of the Faith No More Cultural and Theological Center."

James Martin, one of the titans of twentieth-century music, stepped from the booth. "Station," he said.

"Station," responded the class, much in awe that the driving genius of no less a band than Faith No More stood before them.

Rufus introduced the last guest lecturer. "And, from the twenty-third century, Miss Ria Paschelle, inventor, as you know, of the statiophonic oygenetic amplifiagraphiphonideliverberator. Hard to imagine a world without them."

Paschelle stepped from the phone booth and stationed.

"Who's got a guitar?" asked Rufus.

"I have, Rufus," said a student from the back of the class.

"Excellent! Johann and James have put their heads together and have come up with a little number. Maybe we can get them to play it for us later. Kind of a speed metal concerto . . . But before the class begins, I have a couple of announcements. Remember—Friday: Ben Franklin and Aretha Franklin will be here. And on Saturday we've got the field trip to ancient Babylonia. We've got the hanging gardens booked for 431 B.C sharp. Also—important—as always, no homework—ever—without your headphones on. Got it?"

The class got it.

"Good. Okay, yesterday we were talking about the disposition of the incipient angle and its relationship to harmonic dissonance. Thomas, you want to take it from here?"

Thomas Edison stepped forward, his glasses perched on the end of his nose. He glanced at his notes. "The incipient angle and harmonic dissonance are totally non-heinous—I think we all agree on that. But—and a very big but—"

Rufus's class never got a chance to find out what that big but was, because suddenly the doors of the classroom flew open and De Nomolos's rebels crashed into the room, bursting with menace, like a crack commando team. A group of them trained their weapons on the terrified students, one corralled Bach and Edison, another put a gun to Rufus's throat.

Then De Nomolos swept into the room like a conquering general. On either side of him were two figures, heavily draped in dark, hooded robes.

For a second, even a totally triumphant dude like Rufus could only gape. When he managed to find his voice he could only stammer.

"De Nomolos! My old teacher . . ."

"Rufus," said De Nomolos, his voice heavy with contempt. "My favorite student."

Rufus was still stunned. "I thought you were . . ."

"Dead? No. Just . . . in preparation. I worked within the system until I could stand it no longer. But soon this system will never have existed . . ."

"You won't get away with it," spat Rufus.

"Time will tell."

"Time *has* told."

De Nomolos nodded toward the telephone booth. "I will go back and change that."

"You? You could never change the future, not by yourself."

"And who said anything about doing it by myself? Rufus, you surprise me . . . I have a secret weapon. *Two* secret weapons, in fact." De Nomolos snapped his fingers, and the two hooded figures flanking him threw off their cloaks. Rufus and the class gasped, unable to believe their eyes.

Bach was surprised too. "Was is los?" he asked Edison.

Standing in the middle of the room, bobbing excitedly, were Bill and Ted. They waved to all present.

"How's it goin', dudes!"

"Wilhelm *und* Ted!" said Bach.

"Impossible!" said Rufus. "Bill and Ted would never work for you, De Nomolos, you are totally too non-non-heinous."

"I wouldn't want them," snapped De Nomolos. "Those . . . those *imbeciles* . . ."

De Nomolos's crew knew their cue. "Morons," they muttered, "cretins, idiots . . ."

"Then how?" demanded Rufus.

De Nomolos snapped his fingers. Bill and Ted nodded and grabbed their lower lips and yanked their skin, pulling it off their faces, revealing an elaborate patchwork of intricate wiring and circuitry. The students stared, their mouths agape. One even passed out, and that seemed to please De Nomolos. Bill and Ted pushed their skin back into place.

"So you see, Rufus, I have laid my plans very carefully. These automatons, my old student, are replicas only, programmed with my agenda." He turned to the Evil Bill and Evil Ted. "Now. What is your mission?"

"Okay," said Evil Bill, "first we totally kill Bill and Ted."

"Yah," said Evil Ted. "Then we totally take over their lives."

"Whooooooaaaaa!" said Evil Bill delightedly. "Then we utterly destroy them!"

"Yah. Then at the Battle of the Bands . . .we give the speech they were gonna give."

"De Nomolos," said Rufus soberly, "you cannot ruin that Battle of the Bands. It is too important to all of us. To the future history of the world."

De Nomolos chuckled. "There shall be a *new* future. A new future will be born. A great future, eh?"

"Don't tell us," said Evil Bill, "*you* programmed *us*."

"Yah," said Evil Ted, "he's totally a robot!"

"So are you, dude!"

"We're total Metal Heads!"

The air was split with a long, wild riff of air guitar.

"Silence!" ordered De Nomolos. "That, I am thankful to say, is a sound whose time is fast disappearing." He fixed a stern eye on his men. "What is the fuel?" he demanded like a tough school teacher.

"Fear," said his henchmen.

"What is the engine?"

"Discipline," they answered obediently.

"What is the ideal?"

"Order."

De Nomolos turned to Evil Bill and Evil Ted and stared intently at them. "And how shall we achieve it?"

The robots were well trained. Instantly, they put on their shades and stepped into the phone booth. They spoke in unison. "Death to Bill and Ted."

"Exactly!" said De Nomolos, smacking one hand into the other. "Now, go do your master's bidding."

"Later, dude!" said Evil Ted.

Rufus had taken advantage of the shift in attention and grabbed the guitar from his student. As the phone booth began to disappear into the floor in a great shower of sparks and smoke, he hooked the instrument onto the edge of the booth's antenna.

"Stop him!" yelled De Nomolos.

Suddenly, the room was alive with wild gunfire, the shrieks of the terrified students and the loud, characteristic "Whoaaaa" of Bill and Ted, evil or otherwise, disappearing into the

Circuits of Time. When the smoke cleared, they were gone. And so was Rufus.

De Nomolos's eyes blazed with anger. "You fools. You let him escape!"

The henchmen hung their heads, wondering if their master was on the verge of giving the order that they open fire on one another.

"He cannot succeed," growled De Nomolos. "I will *not* permit it. Do you understand me? They will be destroyed, those, those . . . evolutionary mistakes!"

"Birdbrains . . . imbeciles," said the henchmen dutifully.

"I must prevail. I must prevail because *history has already been written*." He grabbed a book from one of his men and held it aloft, seeming to threaten the students with it. "Have you any idea what this kind of thing costs?" It was a textbook decorated with a hugely overblown picture of De Nomolos. The title told the whole story: *Nomolos de Nomolos—The Greatest Man in History*.

Johann Sebastian Bach rolled his eyes. "*Schiessemunt*."

De Nomolos whipped around and pointed at him. "You! Detention!"

Chapter 2

Not even Bill and Ted's biggest fans would say that at this stage of their development they were the most gifted musicians in the world. The Wyld Stallyns were still growing musically— and that was a kind way of putting things— and even Bill and Ted knew that there was room for improvement. Joanna and Elizabeth were on drums and keyboards, and they were pretty good—music was a big babe thing in the fifteenth century—and Bill and Ted had taken a few lessons, so things were looking up. Still, as musicians they remained on the wrong side of triumphant. Bill knew it, Ted knew it, the girls knew it and, unfortunately, Mrs. Wardroe, a major power in the San Dimas music scene, was about to find out about it too.

She was auditioning Wyld Stallyns for a Battle of the Bands she was putting together, and Bill and Ted were desperate to make the cut. They were not doing well, but Rianna Wardroe was determined to hear them to the end, which was pretty excellent of her, considering.

When they finished their set, Bill leaped to the microphone and managed to make himself heard over the feedback that wailed through the auditorium.

"Thank you! Hope we did okay for this audition. I'm Bill S. Preston, Esquire. This is Ted "Theodore" Logan . . ."

Ted did a lame little riff on his guitar and spoke into his mike. "And on drums and keyboards, celebrating their fifth year in this century are the beautiful princesses from Medieval England—Joanna and Elizabeth. And we are Wyld Stallyns!"

The four "musicians" stared hopefully at Mrs. Wardroe. She stared back. Then Bill realized something was missing.

"Ted," he stage-whispered, "close the show, dude."

Ted slapped his forehead. "Finally, in closing, we just wanted to say . . . uh . . ." He had worked out a speech beforehand, but he couldn't remember it. "Okay, a lotta times you feel . . . you *feel* . . ." He looked panic-stricken to Bill. "Dude, take it . . ."

Bill was no better prepared. "Okay, see, well, like he said . . . love is . . . is . . . nice?"

There was silence and the stage lights snapped off abruptly. Then, from the back of the auditorium, Mrs. Wardroe started clapping, slowly. Bill and Ted suspected she might not have been sincere, but they made the best of the applause.

"Well," Ted whispered, "at least she's not booing us."

Mrs. Wardroe walked down to the front of the theater and stood with her arms folded across her considerable chest, appraising the Wyld Stallyns with a critical eye.

"Okay, first off, your closing speech. It's the lamest thing I've ever heard."

They couldn't really argue with that. "Yah," said Ted. "We know. We totally didn't know what to say."

Mrs. Wardroe shook her head. "I mean, you guys keep telling me you're gonna be the greatest band in the world, but you stink."

"We've noticed that ourselves," said Ted.

"Yah," said Bill. "We don't understand it either."

"You can't sing," said Mrs. Wardroe. "I mean, the girls, they can play, but you guys . . ." She threw up her hands.

"Well," said Bill, "you know girls mature faster than boys? It's a scientific fact."

"Yah. Plus they started playing in the fifteenth century, that's kinda a head start."

Mrs. Wardroe shook her head, as if clearing her brain. "What does that mean? The fifteenth century?"

Ted stepped forward and began explaining earnestly. "See, Mrs. Wardroe, Elizabeth and Joanna are princesses from Medieval England and—"

"Ted," said Bill, "I'm sure Mrs. Wardroe isn't interested in hearing about—"

"Oh. Yah. Right." Ted thought a moment, then his face brightened. "Medieval England, Iowa. They're from Medieval England, Iowa."

"And they're princesses to us," said Bill.

"Yah."

"Look," said Mrs. Wardroe quickly, "it doesn't matter. Guys. The point is the Battle of the Bands is the biggest event for new groups in the area. We're talking about a twenty-five-thousand-dollar first prize."

"Whoaaa," said Bill and Ted.

"*And* a two-year record deal. A chance to be seen by some of the most important people in the business. We've even got live coverage on channel twelve."

"Whooooaaaa," said Bill and Ted. They beamed. Fame and fortune seemed to be finally within their grasp.

"Now, if you guys were me, would you put you guys on?"

Bill and Ted came back to reality with a sickening thud.

"No way," said Bill.

"No way," Ted agreed.

"You see my problem," said Mrs. Wardroe. She paused a moment, then shook her head. "However . . . for some reason, I have faith in you two. So . . . I'm going to give you a shot."

"Excellent!"

"But," she added quickly, "you're going on last. Midnight. By that time everyone should've left."

"That's okay," said Ted, "we're used to it."

"Yah—we fully cleaned out Ted's little brother's junior high school dance."

"They totally turned on 'La Bamba' while Bill was playing his solo. Tough crowd."

"Shut up, Ted."

"Well they did."

"I said shut up, Ted."

Mrs. Wardroe cut in and looked them squarely in the eye. She seemed to be genuinely concerned about them and anxious to help launch their careers, or, at the very least, have them avoid outright humiliation.

"Guys—do yourselves a favor. Prepare a little. Work on your act. Don't embarrass yourselves too badly, huh? I mean you're going to be on TV—it's only local, but you can still make fools of yourselves in front of the whole city."

"Thanks, Mrs. Wardroe," said Bill.

"We won't let you down."

"I hope you don't. Now get out of here. I've got five more bands to audition."

•   •   •

In addition to being non-triumphant musicians, Bill and Ted were now Men of the World. They had jobs—minimum wage at a fast-food joint called Pretzels 'n' Cheese—an apartment of their own, and Bill was the proud owner of a van, a 1985 Ford Econoline van, complete with a hand-painted Wyld Stallyns logo on the side. The van came in handy transporting their equipment to gigs, and the princesses made excellent roadies. While they loaded, Bill and Ted were deep in conversation.

Bill had been doing some thinking, and he had come to a conclusion. "Dude," he announced, "we gotta win that contest."

"Yah," said Ted watching Elizabeth struggling with an amp, "if we win that concert, then we can finally propose to the princesses *and* get some roadies."

"I know. There's no way we can raise a family on the money we make at Pretzels 'n' Cheese."

"Yah. Paying for the princesses' birthday party was hard enough."

"Quiet," cautioned Bill, "they'll hear you."

The birthday party for Joanna and Elizabeth was a most resplendent occasion, considering the state of Bill and Ted's apartment and finances. A banner stretched across the sparsely furnished living room—HAPPY 521st BIRTHDAY JOANNA AND ELIZABETH—and a big picture of the two pretty girls occupied a place of honor among photos of Bill and Ted's other historical friends, like Napoleon, Socrates, Beethoven and the nice-once-you-get-to-know-him dude, Genghis Khan.

The rest of the decoration in the apartment reflected, as you might imagine, Bill and Ted's interest in hard rock. Much wall space was devoted to huge posters of their favorite bands, like Aerosmith, Faith No More and Guns 'n' Roses. What *did* look out of place in the apartment was all the books, most of them devoted to historical subjects—Bill and Ted quite took to history once they started visiting it on a regular basis, and also they wanted to understand what Joanna and Elizabeth were talking about.

You see, although they had been in the modern world for five years and were completely today kind of babes, Elizabeth and Joanna did have the disconcerting habit of occasionally slipping into medieval speak—rood screens and snood caps and boon work and stuff like that—so it was handy to have a book or two around to try and figure out what they were talking about.

Missy, who had the distinction of having been at high school with both Bill and Ted *and* been married to both their fathers—right now she was married to Ted's Dad, Captain Logan—had put most of the party together. Neither Bill nor Ted could quite figure her out—never mind that she was only a year or two older than both of them and was a totally resplendent babe into the bargain—the fact that she had been stepmother to both of them was, to put it mildly, a little confusing.

Captain Logan wasn't confused by his pretty young wife. He was totally in love with her and went around all day with this "How could this have happened to a toad like me?" look on his face. He could barely take his eyes off of her long enough to wish Elizabeth and Joanna a happy birthday and to offer grudging congratulations to his son.

"So . . . I understand you two have a little something else to celebrate tonight." Captain Logan's eyes traveled across the room to his wife.

"We got into the Battle of the Bands," said Elizabeth, Ted's babe. She spoke in a soft English accent.

"Yah," said Ted. "If we win, I can pay you back some of the money I owe you."

Captain Logan did not look impressed. It was hard to impress a cop at any time. It was even harder if you were Ted, his son, and you were trying to impress your father, the police captain, with promises of success with a band he couldn't stand to even hear about, never mind listen to.

"And what if you don't win? Then what?"

Ted thought for a moment. "Well, I guess . . . maybe we'll have to go back to full-time at Pretzels 'n' Cheese. Maybe sell some more blood."

"Maybe you should think about selling a couple of instruments."

"But then what would we play in the band, Dad? You can't have a band without instruments."

"Ted, your band is never going to amount to a hill of beans. And neither will you if you don't get some kind of responsible job."

"Job . . ." said Ted with a shudder.

"You could always come to us, Ted," a voice boomed behind him. Ted turned, his eyes widened and he gulped. The man was dressed in the uniform of a full colonel in the army. Above the left breast pocket of his tunic was a nameplate. It read: "Oats." Ted had once come dangerously close to being packed off to Colonel Oats's military academy in Alaska. He had managed to avert such a dreadful fate, and although Oats seemed bluff and hearty, friendly even, Ted didn't trust him.

"How's . . . how's it going, sir?"

"Splendidly. Remember, it's not too late for you. Or any of you." He winked broadly at Elizabeth. "Plenty of career opportunities in the military for the, uh, weaker sex." He winked again and then pulled Bill and Joanna into the circle. "How about you two?"

"Well, we have other plans, Colonel."

"A band," said Captain Logan derisively.

"A brass band? Plenty of those in the service, son."

"We're a little more interested in rock," said Bill. "Heavy metal."

"Plenty of that too. We call it armor."

"Hi, Oatsie," said Missy, coming up to the little group. She carried a plate in her hand. "Fudge?"

"Love some," said Oats.

Bill tried real hard to sort out a tangled skein of marriages and divorces in an attempt to get his exact relationship to Missy correct. He failed. "How's it goin', Missy, I mean Mom, no . . . wait . . ."

It didn't much matter, as Missy wasn't paying attention. Captain Logan had pulled his wife into a bear hug, and they were kissing deep and long, oblivious to the stares of Elizabeth, Joanna, Bill and Ted.

"I can't believe Missy divorced your dad and married mine," Ted whispered.

Bill shook his head in disbelief. "I know. What's next?"

"Maybe you," said Elizabeth, teasing.

"Yah, then you'll be your own stepdad. You could use the car whenever you wanted."

"That would be most unrivaled," Joanna observed.

Missy managed to pull herself free of Ted's dad, gulped for air and turned to the two princesses. She took a book from her bag and handed it to Elizabeth. "I got this for you. I hope you like it."

Elizabeth read the title on the cover. "*Past*

Lives, Past Lessons. What does that mean?"

Missy looked very serious. "You know, I believe what you say about having lived in Medieval England." Missy lowered her voice. "You see, I understand all about past lives. I used to be Ty Cobb."

"But you're not anymore," said Captain Logan, enfolding her in another squeeze, followed by a kiss.

There was something about all this that struck Bill and Ted as totally bogus.

By the time the party was over and everybody except Joanna and Elizabeth had left, Bill and Ted knew that this was going to be a very important night. Nervously, Ted swallowed hard.

"I hope you liked your party."

"It was lovely," said Elizabeth.

"Resplendent," agreed Joanna.

"But you've probably noticed we haven't given you our gifts yet," said Ted.

"That's because . . . well . . . what we wanted to say . . ."

Bill faltered, and he looked panic-stricken to Ted.

"Actions speak louder than words, dude," Ted said. With that they both dropped to one knee in front of their respective princesses. They produced pieces of paper.

"I wrote this myself," said Bill.

"And I wrote mine," said Ted. "Last night."

Bill cleared his throat. "Joanna . . . as I wander through this dark and lonely forest of life, surrounded by various beasts, like, uh, bears, vipers, squirrels, not to mention small tree-growing lichen, woodpeckers, tree rats, toads, slugs, Gila monsters—Oh no, that's the desert, not the dark forest of life . . ." His pretty speech ground to a halt, but Joanna continued to smile pleasantly, even though she was a bit mystified.

Ted took up the slack. "Elizabeth, as I swim through this dark and fearful sea of existence, surrounded by various creatures: sharks, eels, mahimahi, yellowtail, not to mention tiny barnacles and plankton, man-o'-wars, starfish, blowfish, catfish—Oh no, that's fresh water . . ."

Joanna and Elizabeth were beginning to suspect that there had been a degree of collusion in the writing of these speeches.

"But the point is," said Bill earnestly, "I know we promised you a better life than this . . . Although stuff hasn't actually worked out the way we thought . . . It will . . . I mean, I'm sure that . . . You see . . ."

"Yah," said Ted. "I realize that when we took you out of England we said the future held some really good stuff . . . It will . . . I mean, I'm sure that . . . You see . . ."

"We hope," said Bill.

"We hope," said Ted.

"What are you boys trying to say?"

Bill took a deep breath. "What this is about is . . ."

"The day after tomorrow," said Ted, "if things work out triumphantly . . ."

In unison, they said, "Will you marry us?"

Both girls burst into delighted smiles. Joanna took Bill's hand in hers. "I would love to, Bill."

Elizabeth kissed Ted. "I would be honored . . ."

Bill and Ted looked at each other, not quite able to believe that this was actually happening to them. There was only one response—a long, wild air guitar riff—and the lyrics were obvious: Things couldn't be going much better.

Except.

Elizabeth and Joanna were very old-fashioned girls, and engaged or not, they would not stay the night with their husbands-to-be. Bill and Ted watched from the balcony as the girls drove off in their little convertible Volkswagen—the princesses had better jobs than Bill and Ted, and, consequently, more money. Bill had a thought.

"Dude."

"What?"

"Maybe after we're married, the princesses'll stay over with us."

"Yah. Our girlfriends are most chaste."

Bill was inclined to be philosophical. "Could be worse though."

"Yah? How's that?"

"They could be dating our dads."

"Good point, dude. Good point."

Just then, the phone began to ring. Bill answered it. He shouldn't have.

Chapter
3

A terrible screaming split the serene night sky on the outskirts of San Dimas as a telephone booth hurtled through the darkness like a missile, trailing sparks in its wake. Abruptly, it slowed, heaved itself upright and dropped, plummeting like an elevator out of control, toward the parking lot of a Circle K convenience store. It hit the ground, narrowly missing a cat, which leaped into the air in alarm, then yowled out into the darkness.

The door of the booth slid open, and Evil Bill and Evil Ted stepped out.

"Whoa," said Evil Bill. "Not bad . . ."

"Right on target, dude."

"Now to work some totally triumphant heinous evil."

"They don't call us Evil Bill and Evil Ted for nothing."

"So what do you think we should do now?"

"Better report in to the master-dude."

"Yah." Evil Ted slapped the back of his head, and his right eye popped out of his head and fell into the palm of his hand.

"We have arrived, dude."

The electronic eye began to glow and shimmer, then there was a burst of static across the pupil, then De Nomolos's image appeared as if on the screen of a tiny TV set.

"Is Rufus with you?" he demanded.

Evil Bill and Evil Ted looked around. The antenna of the booth was slightly damaged, a sign that Rufus must have held on until the warp speed of the booth shook him off.

"Looks like we lost him," said Evil Bill.

"Yah. He's somewhere out there in the Circuits of Time."

De Nomolos seemed to relax. "That is very good news. If he's trapped in the Circuits then he's gone forever."

"Excellent!" said Evil Bill and Evil Ted.

"Now," spat De Nomolos, "the first act of business: destroy their ridiculous, insipid band."

"You got it, dude!"

"Get to work!" ordered De Nomolos. His image vanished from Evil Ted's eye, and the robot poked the eyeball back into his socket and blinked as if to get it working again.

"Phase one is about to begin, Evil Bill."

"Yah. They truly will never know what hit them."

They stepped back into the phone booth and, for once, used it for the purpose it was designed for: They made a phone call. Before dialing, though, Ted said, "Let me make sure this program is working, dude." He cleared his throat as if he were about to sing. "Be excellent to one another and party on . . ."

"Not!" said Bill.

Both of them were speaking in the voices of Joanna and Elizabeth, perfect, soft English accents, which sounded kind of strange coming out of the mouths of two guys. "That De Nomolos is one smart dude," said Bill in Elizabeth's voice.

"Truly resplendent," answered Joanna.

"Make the call, dude."

The real Bill answered. "Hi, Bill," said Evil Ted, "this is Joanna."

Bill was mystified. "Joanna? You just drove away. How'd you get home so fast?"

"It is not important. But this is. Listen carefully: Elizabeth and I have totally talked it over and we have decided we are quitting the Wyld Stallyns."

A number of Bill's past lives seemed to shoot past his eyes. He felt dizzy and sick to his stomach. "What! Why?"

Ted pressed his ear against the earpiece of the phone and listened in amazement.

"Elizabeth and I think you're total losers and we never want to see you again."

"No way!" exclaimed Ted. He didn't feel so hot himself, and his symptoms were remarkably similar to Bill's.

Elizabeth's voice came on the line. "We're leaving you forever. We are going to the desert to be alone and to try and forget we ever knew you."

"But—" protested Bill.

"It's over," said Joanna. "Good-bye." The receiver was replaced firmly, and the line died just about the same time Bill and Ted's entire world expired. Eyes glazed over, they sunk down onto the couch, unable to believe what they had heard.

"Maybe," stammered Ted, "maybe we shoulda proposed to them sooner."

"How could we, Ted? We can barely afford our own apartment, never mind babes and babies."

They hung their heads dejectedly, sadder than they had ever been before in their short, active lives.

Bill more or less summed it up. "This is most non-non-heinous."

"What are we gonna do?" said Ted plaintively. "We can't just give up, just like that . . ."

"We gotta find 'em, we gotta talk to them."

"How? They said they were going to the desert. The desert is a truly large place."

As the enormity of the disaster that had befallen them began to sink in, they felt the weight of the world on their shoulders—it seemed to push them further into the cushions of the couch. Nothing, it seemed, could be worse than this, nothing . . .

Evil Bill and Evil Ted, on the other hand, were ecstatic, delighted with the evil they had wrought—that was, after all, what they had been programmed for.

"Whoaa, dude," said Evil Bill, "we totally fooled those other us's."

"Yah. They're completely brilliant . . . ," said Evil Ted.

Then, in unison, they added gleefully, "Not!"

There were a few seconds of spirited air guitar.

"Okay," said Evil Bill, "let's lose the phone booth and start phase two."

Evil Ted gave a thumbs-up. "Station, dude."

Bill and Ted—the real Bill and Ted—experienced a rush of hope when they heard their doorbell ring. Maybe the soft chimes would awaken them from the nightmare the evening had become.

"Maybe it's them. Maybe they were just . . . ," said Bill.

"Yah! Maybe they were just playing a trick to see if our love was true. Or maybe it was a mistake. Get the door, dude."

Bill wrenched open the door, and his jaw dropped so low it almost clanged on the floor.

He was looking at himself and Ted. He didn't know yet that there were some fundamental differences at play here.

"How's it goin', Bill and Ted?" asked Evil Bill and Evil Ted amiably.

"Ted, it's us. Again."

Bill and Ted looked wide-eyed at each other. Very softly they said, "Whooaaa . . ."

Serious and solemn, Bill shook hands with himself, which is a pretty strange feeling. "How's it goin', Bill?"

"Not bad," said Evil Bill amiably. "You?"

"Bad, dude, real bad."

Evil Bill and Evil Ted nodded understandingly. They actually seemed to pity Good Bill and Good Ted. They were programmed to be good, insincere actors.

"I think I see all the signs here of babe trouble," said Evil Ted.

"Totally heinous babe trouble, Ted," said Ted.

"Well, we came to help you guys in your most unfortunate, non-resplendent situation," said Evil Bill.

"How?"

"Come with us," said Evil Ted, "we'll show you."

"Just a minute," said Ted. "Excuse us a minute, will you, future-dudes?" Bill and Ted huddled in a corner of the living room.

"Dude," Ted whispered, "I got a weird feeling here."

"Why? We said we were going to help us. It's just the kind of thing we'd do for us."

"I dunno . . . How do we know these guys are really us? I mean, we don't actually know us . . ."

They looked over at the two evil ones, who were sitting on the couch helping themselves to the food and drinks left over from the party.

"They look like us," said Bill. "And they act like us. And they know we have most heinous trouble with the princesses."

"I dunno . . . ," said Ted, "it seems kinda strange to me."

"Ted, we've been through this before. If it wasn't for that previous intervention of our future selves, would we have even passed history? Think of it, dude, we might still be in high school if it wasn't for us. We wouldn't even be where we are today, would we?"

"No," said Ted.

"And we never would have met the babes, never mind getting engaged to them, would we? I mean, I admit, it wasn't a long engagement, but it never would ever have happened if it hadn't been for us, would it?"

"No," said Ted.

"Without our intervention last time, would we have ever had a most excellent adventure through time?"

"No," said Ted, "but I still think we should give them some kind of test."

"Okay. You do it."

Ted walked over to Evil Ted. "Okay. Ted. If you're really me . . . how many fingers am I about to hold up?"

"Three," said Evil Ted.

Good Ted looked at his hand as if it had a mind of its own, and sure enough, three fingers popped up. Ted stared at them for a minute and then brightened.

"Whoa. You—I mean me—was right."

"Excellent," said Bill. "They're on the level."

"Of course we are, dude," said Evil Bill. "Would we lie to us?"

All four of them said, "No way!" and air-guitared their way out the door.

Evil Bill and Evil Ted looked exactly like Good Bill and Good Ted, but there were some subtle differences that they noticed right away. Evil Ted was driving the Wyld Stallyns van, pushing the old heap to the limit, driving recklessly and fast, zooming through the quiet night streets of San Dimas, headed for the desert.

Bill and Ted were in the back seat, a little in awe of their other selves. "I had no idea I was a reckless driver," said Ted unhappily. "I'm gonna have to watch that."

"I'm cold," said Bill.

"Yah," said Ted, "me too. Hey, Bill, Ted, could we have the heater on back here?"

Evil Bill turned in the front passenger seat and looked at them darkly. "Shut up, Bill."

Bill and Ted were shocked that they would treat themselves with such lack of manners. They stared, mouths agape.

"Whoa, that you is a real jerk," said Ted.

"Yah. I gotta remember to be more considerate toward myself when I become him."

"He said shut your holes," yelled Evil Ted, not taking his eyes off the road.

Ted had had enough from himself. He leaned forward in direct confrontation with Evil Ted. "What is your problem, dude?"

"I'm not interested in your insipid jabbering, you despicable insect."

"Well, excuse me, Ted!" said Ted, his eyes bugging out in surprise and shock at the way he was treating himself. He was also astonished to learn that he knew the word "insipid."

Bill realized that they were in the middle of a potentially volatile situation, not to mention dangerous—the angrier the other Ted got, the faster and more wildly he drove. It made sense to Bill to try and calm things down, even if it meant dealing with two jerks like themselves.

"Hey," said Bill brightly, "maybe we should stop for some food and talk this—"

Evil Bill turned around in his seat, his eyes burning with fury. "Shut your rotting, stinking heads, vermin."

The heat of his anger instantly cowed Bill and Ted. They sunk down in their seats, their shoulders sagging, as if they were trying to make themselves as inconspicuous as possible.

"Dude," said Ted quietly, "I got a very bad feeling . . ."

Dawn was breaking when Evil Ted turned the van off the road and drove out into the desert. The brown, parched earth seemed to stretch for miles in every direction, unrelieved by any distinguishing features, but Evil Ted seemed to know exactly where they were headed. After twenty dusty miles, some outcroppings of rock appeared on the horizon and grew in size as the van neared. They were making straight for them.

"Uh . . . excuse me," said Bill, "but you think you dudes might like to tell us where we're going?"

"No," snarled Evil Bill, "we dudes wouldn't."

"Oh," said Bill.

Through the long night ride, Ted had been doing some totally serious thinking and he had come to some conclusions. He was not happy about them, but they were obvious and inescapable.

"Dude," he whispered to Bill, "what if these are evil robot us's from the future, sent here to kill us and replace us?"

Bill's answer was emphatic. "Ted, if that were true, it would be the beginning of a most bogus journey."

It was, in fact, the end of a most bogus journey. High in the hills, the van screeched to a halt in a cloud of dust.

"Out," ordered Evil Bill.

Bill and Ted slid back the van door and climbed out slowly, blinking in the sunlight. Bill still had one little shred of hope left. "So," he asked, "where are Joanna and Elizabeth?"

"They're not here," said Evil Ted.

"Yah," said Evil Bill, "we lied. Here's the truth: We're totally going to kill you."

"No way!" said Bill and Ted.

"Yes way, dudes," said Evil Ted. "We're fully programmed to do it."

"Yah," said Evil Bill happily. "Not only that, we *want* to do it too."

This was too much for Bill to take. He stepped forward and punched himself hard in the jaw. "You jerk, Bill!" His knuckles crunched on Evil Bill's face, and he fell back, burying his fist in his stomach. "Ow! You are metal, dude!"

Evil Bill chuckled. "I know! Check it out!" He ripped open his chest, and Bill and Ted stared at the wild tangle of wires and circuits that pulsed under the steel.

"Whooaaaa!"

Evil Ted and Evil Bill were so delighted with their sheer evilness that they couldn't help themselves—they jumped and bobbed and weaved in a wild, exuberant air guitar. Raucous, electric music twanged out and echoed in the rocks.

Then they stopped and turned grimly to their two captives.

"Let's go," they ordered.

"Bogus," said Bill and Ted.

Evil Bill and Evil Ted pushed them toward the edge of the cliff. Bill and Ted looked over the ledge and paled.

"Dude," said Ted, his voice quavering, "this is a totally high cliff."

"We gotta try something . . . anything."

Evil Ted nudged Ted toward the void. "Later, dude," he said with a grin.

"Wait," said Ted, "dudes, even though you're doing this, you should know . . . we . . . we . . . Bill?"

"Yah . . . we . . . we *love* you."

"Yah!" said Ted, relieved. "That's it! We love you."

Evil Bill and Evil Ted exchanged glances, rolled their eyes and smiled cruelly.

"Wimps," they spat. Then they pushed them hard. Bill and Ted never had a chance—they went over the edge, plummeting helplessly into space, their arms and legs windmilling, their wide eyes filled with fear.

"Noooooooooo waaaaaaaaaaaaaaayyyyyyyyyyy!" they shrieked as they fell, the ground seeming to rush up to meet them. Their screams echoed through the canyon, caroming off the rocks.

Evil Bill and Evil Ted stood at the edge of the cliff and watched with satisfaction as Good Ted and Good Bill dropped toward their doom. The screams grew more terrified as they grew fainter; then from far off at the bottom of the canyon came two quick, sickening thumps as Bill and Ted hit hard.

"Excellent!" said Evil Bill and Evil Ted. They high-fived and air-guitared and then headed for the van.

"Wait!" said Evil Bill. "How about a round of loogies?"

"Excellent idea, dude!" Evil Bill and Evil Ted returned to the edge of the cliff and very carefully, with precise aim, dropped two long, ropey skeins of spittle over the side.

"Whooaa!" said Bill exultantly, "I totally loogied on that good dead me!"

"Yah!" yelled Evil Ted. "We're fully evil robots!"

"Yah!" said Evil Bill, breaking into a spirited air guitar.

"Hey, I got a great idea," said Evil Ted.

"Let's hear it, dude."

"Let's dump the van. We'll head back to the highway and steal us a good car."

"A Porsche!"

"Yah! Excellent!"

Chapter
4

At the bottom of the desolate ravine, sprawled in a thicket of dry desert shrubs, lay the limp, lifeless bodies of those excellent friends and totally triumphant dudes Bill S. Preston, Esquire, and Ted "Theodore" Logan, both of San Dimas, California, and late of a mostly non-heinous band called Wyld Stallyns. It was a sad sight for all to behold, except for the vultures who were beginning to gather in the sky high above. They thought it was most triumphant.

The two bodies lay unmoving as dead bodies do, but after a few minutes, two spirits arose, two pale, washed-out black-and-white–looking Bill and Teds stood up and looked down at their former selves.

"Bill, what happened?" Ted rubbed his eyes.

"We were totally pushed off a cliff, dude."

Ted looked up to where they had once stood with Evil Bill and Evil Ted and then followed their path through the air all the way down to his own body sprawled at his feet.

"Whoaa," he said softly.

"I think we have to face facts here," said Bill. "Ted—we're dead, dude."

"No way," Ted whispered.

"Yes way. Just look. Do those bodies look like us?"

"Yah."

"Do they look healthy to you, dude?"

"No."

"Do they even look alive to you?"

The awful truth struck Ted with the force of a weighty cannonball. "We *are* dead, dude."

"Bogus . . . Now what?"

Fate—literally—was about to intervene. Creeping up behind them, clambering over the rocks, was a dude dressed in long black robes and carrying a scythe as long as a deep-sea fishing pole. He was Death and he looked it. You couldn't really make out his features, hidden as they were by the overhang of his hood, but you got the feeling that his face was not something you wanted to look at for too long. The bones of his hands burst through the old, cracked flesh, as if through old gloves, and he held his scythe in a clawlike grip. If his complexion was anything like his hands, the dude was not much in the looks department.

Bill and Ted sensed him before they saw him. Something made the hair on the backs of their necks stand up, and they turned slowly, bug-eyed with fear.

"Who's that?" whispered Bill.

"I dunno, but he's dressed a little warm for the desert."

Death was almost on them now, and Bill and Ted definitely did not like what they were seeing.

"Whoa," said Bill, "maybe he's just passing through, out for a stroll, maybe?"

"Let's hope."

Then an ugly, sickening, terrible realization hit Bill.

"Dude . . . if we're dead, then that must be the Grim Reaper. In person."

Ted was always interested in meeting new people, even under difficult circumstances like this. "The Grim Reaper? Oh . . . how's it hangin', Death?"

The Grim Reaper was in the business of meeting new people—happened every day in his line of work—so he wasn't too impressed with Ted's apparent friendliness. He crooked his bony finger at them, calling them to him.

He spoke very slowly, in a deep voice that seemed to echo from a cold tomb deep in the ground. "You will come with me."

Bill and Ted looked at each other and then back at Death. They were reluctant to obey Death, understandably under the circumstances.

Ted's mind had slipped into overdrive and things were beginning to make sense. "Bill, we can't go with this dude, even if he is who he says he is. We have way more important things to do. We gotta get back to the babes. It couldn't have been them on the phone—it must have been some trick those bad dudes played. That means they still love us. Dude, we *gotta* get back."

"Ted, we can't. We're dead."

"We gotta stop those evil us's. We gotta try, even if it's only for the sake of our reputations—I mean, people are going to go through life thinking that those us's are the real us's and that we're real jerks."

Bill thought it over for a moment. It seemed to make sense, sort of.

He smiled as engagingly as he could at the Grim Reaper.

"Excuse us, dude, but is there any way back to, you know, San Dimas, also known as the land of the living?"

Death rolled his bloodshot eyes. Always the same question, from everybody. No one ever just admitted their fate and said, "Okay, Grim Reaper, you got me."

"Is there?" asked Ted eagerly. "See, we've got totally important things to say to some babes, so if there's a way back, we sure would **appreciate hearing about it.**"

"Yeah, Death-dude, how 'bout it?"

The figure nodded portentously. "There is a way back," he said slowly in that spooky deep voice of his.

"Excellent!" said Bill and Ted.

"What is it?" asked Ted.

"What do we have to do?"

"You may challenge me to a contest . . . But if you lose you will be doomed—"

"Look at us, dude, how much more doomed can we get?"

Death held up his cracked and bony old hand. "If you lose you are doomed to remain here in the afterlife . . . for all eternity." Death paused a moment, then added, "It's no fun, let me tell you."

They took him at his word. The afterlife, what they had seen of it so far, was no day at the beach. Still, the alternatives were worse. At least that's what they were hoping.

Ted swallowed hard. He didn't much care for the odds of two guys who barely graduated from high school challenging a major player like Death to a contest. Still, they didn't seem to have any alternative, so it was best to make the most out of the opportunity. "We could always win, right? I mean, what happens if we win?"

Death smiled his best, icy, Grim Reaper–style smile—his teeth were a mess—and laughed hollowly. "No one has ever won. Put such foolishness from your mind. Now you must come with me." He turned and, using his scythe as a walking stick, started leading the way slowly into eternity.

Ted had seen and heard enough. There had to be an easier way out of this than challenging Death to a contest. "Dude," he whispered to Bill, "we have got to ditch this guy."

Bill and Ted were such triumphant friends mainly because they saw eye to eye about almost everything. Especially this time. "Definitely," said Bill. "But how?"

They were also triumphant friends because they thought almost identically, as if they had only one brain between them—which wasn't really all that far from the truth. They had the same excellent idea in the same split second.

"Melvin!"

They air-guitared for a second—so truly awesome was their idea, they just had to— then they put their truly triumphant plan into action.

"Excuse us, dude," said Ted innocently, "but your shoe is untied."

"Oh," said Death, " 'preciate it." He stopped and put his scythe down on a handy rock and then bent over to tie the leather thong on his ratty old sandal.

That was the only advantage Bill and Ted needed. They rushed the Grim Reaper, and in amongst all the yards of material in his black robes they managed to get hold of his

underwear—lucky for them Death wore boxers—and yanked. From somewhere inside his
flapping hood, all Death had to say about this
alarming turn of events was "Oooooomph!"

It was all over in a matter of seconds. Death
was lying in the dust wrestling with his tangled clothes, and Bill and Ted were on their
way out of there.

"I can't believe we just melvined Death,"
said Ted.

"Let's just hope he doesn't catch up with us."

"We gotta keep moving."

"That shouldn't be too much of a problem,"
said Bill, "not for me anyway."

Ted was already hot—it was the desert,
after all—and he was beginning to run out
of breath. "No?" he said between puffs. "How
come?"

"Because, dude, we got Death on our tail.
And he is not happy."

"Good point, dude, good point." Keeping that
simple thought before them, neither Bill nor
Ted found it hard to keep running all the way
back to San Dimas.

They were surprised to see a Porsche parked
in their space in the parking lot of their apartment building. It was a top-of-the-line Porsche
Carrera, jet black, with a spoiler, air condition-
ing and a triumphant CD system.

"Check this out, dude," said Bill. "In the
future, we'll have a Porsche."

"This is the present, dude. Those evil us's probably stole it."

"Those guys just can't be trusted," said Bill sorrowfully.

"And they're in our apartment." Ted sounded no less sorrowful. "Possibly with the princesses."

"We gotta get up there, dude."

"Yeah, but how?"

"Uh . . . you think maybe our keys still work?"

"Oh. I forgot. I guess it's worth a try."

The keys worked. Bill and Ted slipped the catch on the lock gingerly, as if they were breaking in, although seeing as it was their own apartment, they had a perfect right to be there, dead or not. Besides, they didn't have to worry about making too much noise, because Evil Bill and Evil Ted had the music cranked up high. The whole apartment shook with the music of Faith No More—it was so loud, they could have taken the door out with a bazooka.

The living room was more trashed even than when Good Bill and Good Ted had lived there, but it was empty of people, and robots for that matter.

"Where are they?" Bill asked Ted.

"Let's hope they went back where they came from. That would definitely be a step in the triumphant direction," said Ted.

"Wait." Bill froze in the middle of the living room. "What was that?"

"What was what?"

"*That!*"

It was a short, sharp squeal. Not a squeal of pleasure, but of distress. It was, however, undeniably feminine.

"Elizabeth!" said Ted in alarm.

"Joanna!"

"They're in the bedroom!"

"Whoaa," said Bill. "I didn't know the princesses knew where it was."

"Sssh," said Ted, creeping toward the bedroom door. The door was slightly ajar, just enough for Bill and Ted to peer into their room. They could only gasp at what they saw.

You might say that it had already been a difficult day. First, they ask two girls to marry them and like ten minutes later the babes call it off in the most heinous terms, *then* two evil Bill and Ted robots show up, kidnap good Bill and Ted to the desert, where, most bogusly, they get killed *and* most heinously loogied, then Death shows up to doom them to the afterlife forever. Well, all of that was just a lead up, an introduction to the totally non-triumphant sight that was now before their eyes.

On their own beds were their own babes flirting with Evil Bill and Ted, who were, it must be said, flirting back. Luckily, the babes weren't totally into it, being chaste and true as they were.

Still, it was upsetting, to say the least.

"No way!" gasped Bill.

"Those evil us's are trying to totally score with our future wives," said Ted, aghast.

Evil Bill and Evil Ted tried to grab the girls by the arms, holding the princesses back.

"No!" shouted Good Ted. "Let her go!"

Bill restrained him, hauling him back by the neck of his T-shirt. "Ted! It's no use. They can't hear you."

"C'mon, babe," Evil Bill growled, "it's time to get better acquainted."

"Leave her alone!" yelled Good Bill.

"Dude," said Ted, "*you* just told *me* they can't hear us."

The princesses, however, didn't need protection. They weren't going to take their treatment lying down. Both of them managed to break free, and they stumbled to their feet and looked, furious and hurt, at the two men they thought they loved.

"Come on back here, babe," said Evil Bill to Joanna, "we haven't hardly started yet."

Joanna's answer to Evil Bill was a stinging slap to his cheek.

"Way to go, Joanna!" yelled Good Bill.

But Evil Bill just laughed it off. "I like a woman with a little spark!"

"I don't understand what's come over you two," said Elizabeth fiercely. "You've never acted like this before. You've always been perfect gentlemen . . . almost."

Evil Bill grinned and nodded. "We used to be sissies. But no more babe. *Now* we're metal."

"*Heavy* metal, babes," said Evil Ted.

"So get back here," ordered Evil Bill.

"Elizabeth," said Joanna very coolly, considering, "I think we should go."

"Yes. And you two . . . gentlemen can forget about the two of us playing in your band."

Evil Ted just grinned. The band was history anyway, and even if it weren't, the Wyld Stallyns wasn't much without the superior musicianship of the babes. "That's just fine with us, babe."

"Bill," demanded Joanna, "*is* that what *you* want?"

"*Suuure*, babe."

The two princesses could not believe what they were hearing. These two guys couldn't be the Bill and Ted they knew and loved.

"So this is what life with you would have been like?" said Elizabeth.

"Like this!" said Evil Ted. "And worse!"

"A lot worse," said Evil Bill with a leer.

Joanna and Elizabeth exchanged glances quickly. "Well," said Elizabeth, "that's that, I should think."

"Definitely," said Joanna. "I think we should be going."

Evil Ted shrugged. "Yah. Well, see ya . . ."

Elizabeth stood up very straight. "I hope," she said coldly, "that I never again in my life lay my eyes on Ted 'Theodore' Logan."

"And I hope I never see you again as long as I live, Bill S. Preston, Esquire," said Joanna.

"No . . . way," said Good Bill and Good Ted. Right then it didn't seem to matter which Bill and Ted the princesses were walking out on. If they didn't like Bill and Ted . . . they didn't like Bill and Ted and that was totally heinous news, no matter how you sliced it. Both Bill and Ted, the good ones, knew they had a long, uphill struggle before they could begin to win their beloved babes back.

Evil Bill and Evil Ted didn't seem to care.

"If that's the way you want it, babes . . ." Evil Bill shrugged his shoulders, as if he couldn't care less.

"Yah," said Evil Ted, "guess we'll catch you later, babes."

"I don't think so," said Joanna.

"There will be no later with these babes . . . dudes," said Elizabeth.

The two princesses stalked from the room with all the dignity they could muster. As they passed through the doorway they actually passed through the ghostly forms of Good Bill and Good Ted—a feeling not all that heinous when you came right down to it.

"Whoooaaa," said Bill.

"Elizabeth! Joanna! Wait!" But Good Ted couldn't stop them. A second later he and Bill heard the front door slam.

"They're gone, dude," said Bill.

"I can't believe it."

"Sssh," said Bill, "listen."

Evil Bill and Evil Ted were still sprawled on the beds, and they giggled at the fact that the princesses had left them.

"Who needs them anyway?" asked Evil Bill.

"So high and mighty. Acted like they were too good for us evil robots."

"Dude, no babe can get away with treating me like that. I don't care if they are princesses."

"*Or* even if they're not in love with us, but with those other jerks."

"Right," said Evil Bill. "Listen, I got an idea."

"I'm all ears, dude."

"After the concert, after we make De Nomolos's speech, I say we waste 'em. The two babes. Waste 'em dead."

"No!" screamed Good Bill and Good Ted.

"Yah!" said Evil Ted.

"That'll show 'em."

"Station. For now, let's trash this lame little rat hole. Trash it good!"

"Trashed already," said Good Ted. "Our whole life is trashed . . ."

"No babes," said Good Bill sadly, "without our babes, life is trash."

Evil Ted had jumped off the bed. "I want to scratch the records."

"Stellar, Evil Ted. I'll set fire to the rug."

The Evil Ones dashed out of the room, intent on causing as much trouble as they could in the shortest possible time. Good Ted and Good Bill sank down onto their old beds, dejected and sick at heart.

"No, babes," moaned Bill, "no concert . . ."

"No life," said Ted.

"We can't give up," said Bill. "We have to stop them."

"Yah. But how?"

Bill thought for a moment, which was not easy to do considering the noise of breaking glass and crashing furniture that was coming from the other room.

Suddenly, though, he had a plan.

"Ted," said Bill, "I think it's time we went to the authorities . . ."

With the possible exception of Death and Evil Bill and Evil Ted, the person Good Ted wanted to see least in the world was his father, Captain Logan—and yet he was the authority Bill had in mind.

They got to the San Dimas police station in time for the morning briefing conducted by Captain Logan. He was standing at a podium before the full day shift of the SDPD, fifteen deputies in all, doing his stern cop number. The policemen were taking notes, paying close attention to what their chief had to say. Few took advantage of the coffee and doughnuts supplied by the department.

"Herzfeld," ordered Captain Logan, "I want you to move downtown so Officer Deloach can take her maternity leave."

"Got it, Captain," said one of the cops.

"Also," Logan continued, "tonight we have to make a few shifts. Anyone interested in moonlighting should know that we'll be stepping up security at the amphitheater for the Battle of the Bands."

Deputy James, Logan's second in command and a younger man than him, smiled.

"I hear your son's going to be playing."

"Please," said Logan grimly, "don't remind me. Also—our parking ticket quota is way down, particularly in the following zones . . ." As Captain Logan referred to his notes on the podium in front of him, Bill and Ted wafted into the room, totally invisible to all eyes.

"I hope this works," said Ted nervously. It was kind of scary being in the same room with his dad, even if he had the added security of being dead and invisible.

Bill could only shrug. "Well, it worked in *Exorcist III*. That should mean something."

Ted still looked totally dubious. "So . . . how do we do this?"

"I dunno . . . I've never exchanged forms with anybody before. Why don't you try something?"

"It was your idea. You go first."

"He's *your* dad, Ted."

"Okay . . . okay." Ted shrugged and stepped up behind his father. He touched Logan on the shoulder and instantly Ted vanished, disappearing into him. Captain Logan's face went blank, as if someone had thrown a switch turning off his personality. Then, gradually, like an engine warming up, character came back into his face, only it wasn't Captain Logan's normal self—he looked friendlier, stupider, a goofy look on his face.

"Okay, dudes," he said.

"Ted! Act like your dad, dude."

"I mean . . . I mean, my fellow police officers. The next order of business is that my son Ted 'Theodore' Logan and his excellent friend Bill S. Preston, Esquire, have been murdered and replaced by evil robots from the future."

"You did it, dude!" exclaimed Bill.

Ted gave him a thumbs-up. To the rest of the policemen in the room, however, it only looked as if Captain Logan, now having taken complete leave of his senses, had just given the thumbs-up to an empty spot in the room.

"You totally possessed your dad!"

"Yah," said Ted and fired off a spirited salvo of inspired air guitar.

The room, however, was extremely quiet. The fifteen deputies were staring hard at their chief, wondering which one of them should go and call an ambulance. It was well known that Captain Logan was a little . . . eccentric, but this time he appeared to have gone completely nuts.

Ted did his best to get back into the officious character of his father. "Okay. You gotta go over and arrest these robots so they don't ruin everything for me and Bill—I mean, my son and Bill—and, most importantly, make sure they don't hurt the babes, uh, princesses, uh . . ."

"Captain," said Deputy James very slowly, as if not to startle the man into doing anything violent, "wouldn't you like to maybe lie down for a little while? Then I think there is a nice doctor over at County General Hospital you might want to have a little chat with." He smiled at Logan, as if promising a lollipop to a child. "How does that sound?"

"This isn't working," whispered Ted. "You gotta back me up, dude."

"You got it, dude," said Bill. Bill stepped up behind Deputy James, touched him on the shoulder and vanished into him. Just as with Captain Logan, James's face went blank and then came back to life, only this life belonged to Bill.

He beamed at Captain Logan. "I totally believe you, dude. We gotta get all the men out to stop those evil robot dudes."

"Oh no," said one of the cops. "Somebody call the cops."

"Whooaa!" said Bill. "Look, dude! Dough-nuts!"

"Excellent!" said Ted.

The two figures almost dived into the box of doughnuts on the briefing table and began stuffing sweet dough into their mouths, oblivi-ous to the entire roomful of cops.

"Savory cruller," said Bill, spraying crumbs all around.

"Yah! I got really hungry being dead."

"Now we're eating, but these aren't even our bodies."

Suddenly Ted remembered where he was—and *who* he was. He looked from face to horrified face. "Dude," he said, suddenly earnest, "this is really weird."

Bill too looked around the room. "Yah."

"Bill. I don't think they believe us."

"Well we've gotta find somebody who will."

Ted chewed a little more doughnut and swallowed. "Wait—it's Saturday, right? Maybe Missy can help us."

"Yah. We gotta get over there."

Ted waved to the policemen. "Catch you later, cop-dudes!"

"Ted! We can't go like this."

"Oh. Yah."

With that, Bill and Ted stepped out of their host bodies and headed for the door. Captain Logan and Deputy James stood dazed in the middle of the room, doughnut crumbs all over their faces. They knew something had happened . . . but they just weren't sure what exactly.

"Where . . . where was I?" stammered Captain Logan.

"Parking tickets," said one of the cops.

Chapter
5

As if there weren't enough weirdness in San Dimas already, Missy, present and past step-mom to either Bill or Ted, had recently gotten heavily into New Age stuff—she believed that gods and goddesses walked the earth, that crystals had the power to heal and zap you full of all kinds of good positive stuff, that the souls of ancient beings dwelled in some specially chosen people and that they could channel those life forces back into the present world. None of this is all that difficult to believe, if you've been keeping up with Bill and Ted's adventures.

Missy was a little more traditional in her approach to past lives than Bill and Ted—no time travel for her. Instead, every Saturday she and five or six of her friends got together, drank herbal tea, listened to New Age music (John Boswell's "Kindred Spirits" was a big crowd pleaser) and tried to get in touch with the spirit world. So far, they hadn't had much luck, but they kept at it gamely. By the time Bill and Ted got to Missy's that morning, the séance was already well under way, and she and her fellow believers were having their usual lack of success.

The Logan living room had been converted into a New Age den. The windows had been heavily draped in red fabric, allowing only a little rosy light to filter into the dim room. Wind chimes tinkled, and music crept softly from speakers more accustomed to Ted's musical tastes. Six or seven men and women sat on cushions in a circle. They held hands and had their eyes shut tight as if concentrating powerfully.

"Ghandi," said one woman.

"Aristotle," said another.

"Anne Boleyn," said one of the two men.

So far, pretty predictable choices, but no one was surprised when the woman next to Missy announced, "President Chester A. Arthur."

"Clark Gable," said the other man.

"Charlemagne . . ."

Missy spoke firmly. "And I would like to contact the spirit of Ty Cobb."

All seven of them started to sway and chant

quietly, a free-form incantation that didn't seem to do much—it certainly wasn't bringing forth any spirits.

Bill and Ted watched from the doorway of the room. "Has this channeling stuff ever worked?" Bill asked.

"No. But it will today, dude."

"How do you know?"

"*We're* spirits, aren't we, dude?"

"Yah, but how will they see us? The cops down at the station didn't see a thing."

"Totally true, but those dudes weren't in the right frame of mind. These people are primed to see us. Besides, they aren't going to see us so much as sense our spectral aura."

"Oh. Why didn't you say so?"

When the incantation was done, Missy took over—she seemed to be pretty much the leader of this bunch. "Oh, great spirits from the netherworld, leave your celestial abode and speak upon us with your life lessons . . . "

"That's us, dude," said Ted. There was a slight hissing sound, as if the room had been invaded by snakes, and both Bill and Ted rose slowly off the ground, shimmery bluish forms, floating up to the ceiling like balloons at a birthday party.

Missy and her friends stared, their mouths agape. Although they definitely considered themselves believers in the spirit world, somehow they never actually thought they would have any success at channeling, particularly with Missy as their guide.

Missy had experienced doubts before too, but now that it was happening, she had no option but to go through with it and lead her little band. "I . . . I . . . feel the spirits have arrived among us. Welcome, great spirits of the netherworld."

Bill and Ted's voices were hollow and reverberating, spooky, though their message was not. "How's it goin', New Age dudes?"

"Spirits . . . ," said Missy nervously, "can you hear me?"

"Yah," said Ted, "and we can totally see you—"

"It's your mom, Ted," said Bill, alarmed. "But you're right. Move over, dude!" Bill's ghostly spirit tried to jostle Ted's out of the way to get a glimpse of Missy and her friends.

"What have you to say to us, spirits . . . What messages do you bring us from the other side?"

"Oh, we got a lot of news," said Ted. "Listen up. Okay, see the princesses are in trouble with these two evil robot dudes and—"

"Yah!" said Bill, interrupting. "And that's not all. Your son and his excellent friend Bill were killed!"

Missy screamed and her friends were thrown into panic.

"Yah," said Ted, "it was totally heinous."

"You must go!" screamed Missy.

"No, no, not yet! Listen to us. Beware of the

Evil Bill and the Evil Ted. Warn the princesses about them!"

Missy snatched up one of her occult books and began reading a spell quickly. "Oh, evil spirits from Hell—I send you back to the darkness from which you came—"

"No! Missy! You're making a mistake!"

"Totally!"

But Missy was frightened out of her wits. All she or any one of them wanted now was to get rid of these visions they had so unwisely conjured up.

"D'lrow eht elur," she chanted in a low voice, "l'liw sirc d'na de."

"What's she doing?" asked Ted.

"I dunno, dude, but I don't think it's good for us."

"Kaer b'a us't uc!" Missy chanted frantically. Then she slammed shut her book.

The hissing in the room grew louder and louder until it was a great, rushing whoosh of air, sucking at Bill and Ted, pulling them down through the floor, as if down a cosmic drain.

"Noooo waaayyyy!" Bill and Ted shrieked as a black hole opened up at their feet. They shot down into it and the floor closed over them, the only sign that they had ever been in the living room a little burn mark on Missy's carpet.

The hole was dark and endless, and Bill and Ted plummeted faster and faster into the void, screaming uncontrollably—for a little while, anyway. After a while they got to sort of like the feeling so they stopped screaming and, as they continued to fall, looked at each other.

"Dude," said Bill, pleasantly, "this is a totally deep hole."

"Yah." Ted looked down but could see no end in sight. "Now what?"

"I dunno."

"Think we'll ever stop falling, dude?"

"Could take a while."

"What shall we do to pass the time?"

"Twenty questions?" suggested Bill.

"Sounds good . . . I got one."

Bill thought about it for a moment. "Are you a mineral?"

"Yah."

"Are you a tank?"

"Yah. Good one. And you still had eighteen questions to go. Kind of a boring game, though."

"Sort of like this fall." Bill yawned.

"Yah. How about this: knock-knock."

Bill loved a good knock-knock joke. He liked to figure them out. "Who's there?"

"Wyld," said Ted.

"I give up. Wyld who?"

"Wyld Stallyns, dude!"

They were just gearing up to air-guitar when they landed, and they landed lighter and easier than you would have thought considering how far they fell. They hit a giant, smoking, blisteringly hot rock—the thing was the size of a bus—and bounced a couple of times, but it didn't hurt. It must have something to do with being a spirit.

They lay there a second or two, stunned, then slowly got to their feet, dusting themselves off.

"Whoa . . . not bad."

"Yah. I wonder who we talk to about doing it again."

Then they began to look around them. It was hard to tell if they were inside or outdoors—they probably would have guessed in a cave of some sort, a big one, a vast, infinite one that stretched away to the horizon. It was littered with giant, smoking rocks just like the one they were standing on, and the air was thick with smoke and fumes. A chorus of moans and the steady thud of hammers split the noxious air.

"Hell!" said Ted.

"No way . . . ," said Bill.

"This is not what I expected this place to look like at all."

"Yah," agreed Bill. "We got totally lied to by all those album covers."

"Totally!"

"Ted, look!" Bill pointed into the fumes. "Someone's coming. Sort of like a demon-dude. We'll ask him how we get—"

An enormous red pitchfork slammed into the rock, between Bill and Ted, the force throwing them to the ground. When they had picked themselves up again, a giant demon—dressed in a red work apron and wearing a visor, looking like a devil-blacksmith—was standing over them. Without a word he dropped two huge sledgehammers on the rock in front of them.

"Non-non-non-triumphant," said Bill and Ted slowly.

The demon pushed them toward a pile of rocks and pointed, first at the hammers and then at the boulders. Bill and Ted stared blankly at him. Agitatedly, the demon pointed again, first to the rocks, then to the sledgehammers, then back to the rocks.

"I think he wants us to break the rocks with the hammers," said Ted after a moment to consider the meaning of the demon's actions.

"Why would he want us to do that?"

"I dunno, but do you want to argue with him?"

"No way," said Bill.

"Let's break the rocks. Maybe he'll get a little friendlier."

They hefted their hammers. Bill hit a rock. Ted hit a rock. Then Bill again. Then Ted.

"Dude," said Ted, "look, I totally broke a rock."

"Way to go!" said Bill.

The demon nodded and sort of smiled, and they began to get the feeling that maybe, as demons went, he wasn't such a bad dude.

They broke a few more rocks, just to get on his good side. Rock breaking seemed to be the demon's thing. To Ted's surprise, it seemed to be his too.

"You know, Bill, I kinda like this."

"You wanna do it for all eternity?"

That was a tough one. Ted thought a moment. "No," he said with an air of finality.

"Me neither," said Bill. "In fact, I haven't quite taken to it the way you have. How about we quit?"

"Yah."

Bill tapped the demon on the shoulder. "Excuse me, Mr. Demon sir, but how long we gotta do this for?"

"Yah. It's been fun, but we have to get back to San Dimas. It is most urgent."

"We'd love to stay . . . ," said Bill, trying to avoid hurting the demon's feelings.

The demon stuffed one of his hands into his own mouth and pulled out a giant black rat. Holding it by the tail, he dangled the creature in front of the guys' faces.

"Whooaa!" they said, thrilled at such a feat.

"Not bad!" said Bill, full of admiration for anyone capable of pulling large black rats out of his own mouth. Such a skill would have come in quite handy in high school—and he was already thinking of ways of working it into the Wyld Stallyns' act.

"We totally knew this guy, in San Dimas, you know," said Ted, "and he like got one of those in a bucket of chicken. Deep fried."

"This is better, though," said Bill.

"Do something else, dude," urged Ted.

"Yah! Do the rat thing again!"

The guard shook his head and slowly pushed them back to their rock pile and pointed.

"Okay, okay, we know. Break the rocks, right?"

The demon nodded, and Bill and Ted had no choice but to return to their labors.

Ted didn't mind all that much. "Dude, I'm telling you, I like this."

"Ted, you can break rocks when you get home. You can go into the rock breaking business."

"Yah . . . I suppose, but I think I'd maybe rather keep it as more of a hobby."

After a while, Bill stopped to wipe the sweat from his forehead. He looked around and saw, high up in the vault of the cave, a hideous stone sculpture—whoever decorated the place went very much for the rock look—a gargoyle, half-man, half-dragon,, and standing atop this creature was a towering figure, the head man himself, surveying his evil domain.

"Ted, dude, check this out."

"Who's that?"

"Ted. Who do you *think* it is?"

Slowly the truth dawned on him. "Whooaa . . . We gotta get his attention, Bill. He's the dude who can get us out of here and back to San Dimas."

They looked at each other for a moment. "Sign of the Devil, Dude!" Bill and Ted thrust their arms back and forth, index and little fingers raised in the Sign of the Devil, so beloved of right-thinking fans of heavy metal the world over.

"Down here, dude!"

"Yah! We are totally signaling you, dude."

The Evil One noticed and pulled a lever at his side. Suddenly, there was the sound of the grinding of machinery, and slowly Bill and Ted's rock began to rise toward the gargoyle. They clambered off their rock onto the nose of the statue and across its red stone back to the base of a hazy red stairway that led to the throne.

"So," said Bill, "how's it goin', Beelzebub?"

"Excellent rocks," put in Ted.

"We totally broke some."

"Totally."

This did not seem to impress Beelzebub overly—which was not surprising, considering the amount of rock breaking activity that went on in his domain on a daily basis.

"So," said Ted, "we broke the rocks . . . so . . . okay. Can we go now?"

"Yah, 'cause, see, this is all a mistake. It all started with my ex-stepmom—"

"Who's now *my* stepmom—"

"Yah. See, she—" That was as far as they got with their explanation. Their flow of words was cut short by a low, heavy chuckling—he laughed just the way you'd expect him to.

His voice was low too, crackling, as

if fire itself could talk. "I . . . know . . . all . . . about . . . you."

"You *do*?"

"Does that mean . . . ?"

The voice chuckled again. "You . . . may . . . go."

"Thanks, dude!" exclaimed Ted.

"Yah, you know, you got a bad rap, but I gotta say that to me you seem like an okay dude."

"Totally. Now how do we get out of here?"

That was the simple part. A trapdoor opened at their feet, and they fell through the floor, not as far as last time—in fact, the fall was over in seconds—and they knew it because they landed with a thud.

"Whooaa, dude, this has been some kind of day . . ."

"Yah. And now what?"

They were standing in a circular room with small doors like the openings to caves set in the wall, running all the way round, dozens of different passageways radiating out of the chamber like the spokes of a wheel.

"Where are we?" asked Ted.

"I don't know. But I guess we should try one of these doors."

"What else can we do?"

They crept through the nearest passageway, crouched low and moving cautiously. It was like being in a maze, a labyrinth of tunnels and more doors.

"Dude, where are we now?"

"Let's try one of these doors."

They stepped out of the labyrinth and into what seemed to be an army bunker. The walls were concrete, and bits of military equipment were scattered around. It was also freezing, snow sweeping along the hard floor of the bunker.

"*Now* where are we, Bill?"

Bill didn't know, but they found out soon enough. There was a piercing, shrill blast from a whistle, which made the guys jump about six feet in the air. That was bad enough, but even more frightening was the figure clad in green combat fatigues who was striding toward them.

"I know that guy," said Bill.

So did Ted, all too well—as well as he wanted to. "It's totally Colonel Oats!"

Together they said: "No waaay!"

This wasn't the nice Colonel Oats of the princesses' birthday party, old friend to Captain Logan and connoisseur of Missy's cooking, this was the *real* Colonel Oats, the meanest, toughest military commander they had ever met since the last time they said good-bye to their old pal Ghenghis Khan.

Oats eyeballed them malevolently. "Gentlemen!" he barked. "Welcome to Hell!"

"No way!" yelled Ted.

Oats leaned down and screamed in Ted's face, the veins on his neck bulging out. "What did you say to me, you little worm?"

Ted swallowed hard. "No way . . . sir?"

"I am in command here, maggots, and from now on you will do whatever I tell you to do! Is that clear?"

"Yes, sir, dude, sir!" yelled Bill.

"What?" shrieked Oats.

"Yes, sir, dude, sir!"

"*What!*"

Bill took another stab at it. He couldn't see what he was doing wrong. "Yes, sir, sir, dude?" he said hopefully.

Oats pointed at the stone-cold floor. "Get down and give me infinity."

Bill and Ted dropped to the floor and started doing their push-ups. Ted was thinking that they didn't know when they had things good—back there breaking rocks.

"You stupid, pathetic, craven, worthless little cretins!" screamed Oats. "You pitiful, ignorant, flabby little morons! You make me sick!"

"Kinda personal, isn't he, dude?" said Bill unhappily.

"Dude. There is totally no way I can do an infinity of push-ups."

"Maybe if he lets us do 'em girls style . . ."

"No chance, dude. We gotta get out of here—"

"Agreed, dude!"

They jumped to their feet, pushed past the still-screaming Colonel Oats and made a break for the door. They ran down the long labyrinth corridor, completely unaware of where they were headed.

They ran for a few minutes; then it dawned on them that Colonel Oats hadn't caught up—maybe he wasn't even following them. Ted slowed, then stopped, leaning against the rock wall and gasping for breath.

"Dude . . ."

"Ted?"

"I think we're in our own personal Hell . . ."

"And here I always thought it was Geometry class . . ."

"Worse, much worse . . . Bill?"

"Yeah?"

"You know how in the movies, like *Friday the 13th* and *Night of the Living Dead*, you know how someone always says, 'Let's split up' and we're in the audience going totally, 'No, no, dudes, don't split up, how can you be so totally stupid to split up like that?' "

"Yeah?"

"I got an idea."

"*Yeah?*"

"Let's split up!"

"Excellent!

They dove into opposite passageways.

Chapter
6

This is totally true: Those who ignore the lessons of history are doomed to repeat them. And even though Bill and Ted had recently discovered, via time travel and the princesses, that there was something non-heinous to be said for the lessons of history, they still hadn't gotten the hang of things in the doomed-to-repeat-them department.

So first Ted ignores all the history he learned at the movies, the valuable lessons taught by *Night of the Living Dead* and *Aliens*, and splits up, *then* he stumbles back into his own personal history. Bogus move.

The tunnel he had chosen looked, well, like a tunnel for the first few hundred yards, and already he's figuring "piece of cake"—no Colonel Oats, no demon-dude, not even any rock breaking—and then he comes to the staircase. Except, it's not any old staircase; this one looks pretty familiar. And then—whoaaa!— it hits him: This flight of stairs is the one in his own grandparents' house, the one he used to play on when he was a young boy.

At the bottom of the stairs sits a basket, an Easter basket like the kind he used to get when he was a kid, filled with chocolate eggs and that weird green plastic "grass" that got all over the place, plus a couple of those hollow chocolate bunnies wrapped in that tight silver foil that you couldn't ever get all of it off and a little bit would get in your fillings and suddenly your whole mouth felt like an experiment in Science class.

And the weird thing about this basket was that it was marked "To Deacon, Happy Easter from the Easter Bunny." Now, Deacon was Ted's younger, pain-in-the-neck brother, but right at that moment, Ted would have been glad to see even him—that's how desperate he was to get out of this nightmare.

As Ted headed toward the stairs, the strangest thing of that strange day occurred. All of a sudden, Ted was ten years old. Bogus.

Ted rubbed his face and realized that he wouldn't need a shave for . . . well, about ten more years, and just yesterday he had realized he was averaging two a week. He was very confused and frightened.

"What's happened to me?"

He stared down at the Easter basket. Then, suddenly, he grabbed it and stuffed a couple of chocolates into his mouth, his teeth chomping down on the candy, swallowing as fast as he could. The chocolates were good, better than he could ever remember having . . . except on one occasion, ten years before, when he had finished his own Easter candy early and had swiped his brother Deacon's basket figuring "what the hey!" the kid was only three, how would he ever know, right? And until that moment, Ted's crime had been undetected—ten years earlier, his Mom and Dad had bought that lame story he had put out about the dog having eaten it.

But remember that bit about those who ignore the lessons of history being doomed to repeat them? Ted was about to learn the validity of that statement. As he dashed up the stairs, the Easter basket crooked under his arm as if he were a running back, a giant pink and totally heinous, bogus and malevolent Easter Bunny appeared from nowhere, blocking his path.

He pointed a pink furry arm at Ted and said in a voice that was both squeaky and scary, "You took Deacon's Easter basket!"

"That was ten years ago!" screamed Ted.

"*You must pay!*" squeaked the Easter Bunny. He started to hop in a totally evil kind of way that frightened Ted more than all the Deaths, Devils and Demons he had run into that day.

His eyes watched, wide and terrified, as the bunny hopped ever nearer. There was, he realized, only one thing to do: He had to call in reinforcements.

"Bill!" he screamed. "Bill! Help me!"

But Bill had his own problems. In his passageway Bill had come face-to-face with his past and it was scaring him to death. Just as Ted had done, he had started down the tunnel and things were pretty normal for the first few minutes, until he came to a door. The door was at the end of the passageway, and as soon as Bill saw the door he knew—knew!—he shouldn't open it. But some force greater than his own fear compelled him to open it. As the door swung open he came face-to-face with his own worst fear. He was in his grandmother's dining room. But worse than that he was in the dreaded *family reunion in Hell!*

Suddenly Bill was six years old. He had stumbled upon a room filled with all his relatives—Uncle Sid, who always smelled like cigars; Uncle George, who gave the most bogus presents; Aunt Sylvia, who always brought a big gelatin salad and made sure that Bill ate some even though it made him gag; Aunt Nancy, who was always wondering what she'd get in the will—and, in the center of the crowd, the guest of honor, was a tiny old lady . . .

"Bogus," said Bill, his voice quavering in

fear as an expression of sheer terror settled on his face.

"Helloo, little Billy," trilled the old lady.

Bill was barely able to speak. "G-Gr-Granny S. P-P-P-Preston . . . Esquire . . ."

"Isn't he just the cutest little thing!" said Aunt Sylvia, making kissy noises with her heavily lipsticked lips.

"And my, hasn't he grown!" said Uncle George.

"I remember him when he was just this high!" Uncle Sid held his hand about three inches off the ground.

Bill wanted to say he remembered Uncle Sid when he was forty pounds lighter and had all his hair, but the words wouldn't come. His terrified eyes were transfixed by his grandmother's mustachioed upper lip. Soon, he knew, he would hear the words he had dreaded all his life.

His grandmother leaned toward him, and he smelled her makeup and looked away. Otherwise he would have been looking straight down her— He shuddered. Then she spoke:

"How about a kiss for your dear old Granny, little Billy? Kissies for Granny!"

That was it. "Nooo!" screamed Bill and pushed through the crowd of his relatives, fighting his way back to the door, charging down the hall and back out into the labyrinth. He ran smack into Ted. Both of them were pale and breathless with fear, but never had they been so glad to see each other.

"It was horrible!" said Ted.

"Non-non-non-non-heinous!" wailed Bill.

"Dude, we have *got* to get out of here."

Suddenly, the passageway was bathed in an eerie red light and the voice of the Evil One boomed out. "There is no escape! You must choose your eternity."

"And here I thought that society had totally misjudged you!" Bill yelled.

"Yah. They were totally right all the time!"

"You're nothing but the ugly red source-of-all-evil!"

The ugly red source-of-all-evil was silent for a moment as if thinking this over, wondering what he should do next. His next move, when it came, was quite heinous.

The doors of the tunnels flew open, and Bill and Ted's worst fears—Colonel Oats, the evil Easter Bunny and Granny Preston—emerged like monsters in a horror movie.

"Dude! We have totally gotten the devil-dude mad."

They tried to run, but, as if in a bad dream, they moved in slow motion. Bill looked down at his listless legs.

"We're totally NFL Highlights."

"Yah, only this isn't football, it's total eternal damnation and torment."

"That's what happens to dead dudes, dude."

"Then we're going to have to get un-dead.

"Ted . . . I think there's only one way out of here."

"You're right, dude. We gotta play the Reaper."

"Yeah, but where is he? There's never a Grim Reaper around when you need one."

Suddenly, there was a bright flash of light and all was as silent as a tomb.

They were no longer in the tunnels. Instead, they had been transported to a large, empty room, a stark gray-walled chamber that contained nothing except the very calm-looking figure of the Grim Reaper. The Easter Bunny, Granny Preston and Colonel Oats were nowhere to be seen, which was a relief.

"Grim Reaper," said Ted, "are we happy to see you!"

"Yah. You are our last chance."

"You have decided to play me?"

"Totally," said Ted.

The Grim Reaper nodded slowly. "Very well. Choose your game. But if you lose, you will stay here . . . in Hell . . . forever."

"Let me just clear something up with you," said Bill, "are you telling me that Hell is just like life only longer?"

The Grim Reaper nodded.

"I can't believe we're being punished for such . . . little things."

"You took the Easter basket, didn't you?"

Ted squirmed. "Yeah, but . . ."

"Let the games begin," said the Grim Reaper.

Deep in the chamber of the Grim Reaper, Bill and Ted faced Death across a table. They had been playing for what seemed like hours, days maybe, and they felt the tension rise with the passage of every second. Their palms were clammy; sweat beaded on their brows. Death was good . . . very good, a master of the game.

He surveyed the board like a field marshall looking at a battle map. He smiled grimly, then made his move.

"D-1."

Bill and Ted relaxed. "It's a miss," said Bill. The Grim Reaper was a good Battleship player . . . but they were better. A quiet confidence flooded into them.

"Your move," said the Grim Reaper.

"Don't rush us, dude, don't rush us." Bill and Ted conferred quietly for a moment.

"B-3," said Ted.

Grim Reaper chuckled. "Miss."

"Bogus," whispered Bill.

Death fired. "C-6."

"Hit," said Ted grimly.

"Heinous!" said Bill.

"I believe, gentlemen, that this is your final shot."

Bill and Ted nodded grimly, well aware that their total eternal destiny was hanging in the balance.

"Use the Force, Ted."

"Totally, Bill." Ted concentrated harder than he ever had before in his life. This was the shot that counted. "J-7, dude," he said finally.

There was a moment of silence; then the Grim Reaper gritted his cracked old teeth. "Hit. You sunk my battleship."

"Excellent!" yelled Bill and Ted. They jumped from their chairs and wildly high-fived.

"I knew he'd put his battleship in the Js! It's an old trick."

"Good thinking, Ted."

The Grim Reaper was still scowling down at the Battleship game board, stunned that he had actually lost a game. When that got around, he would end up being the laughingstock of the entire underworld. Plainly, he had to do something to defeat these two upstarts and reclaim his lost honor. He looked up and stared balefully at Bill and Ted.

"Time to go, dude," Bill said.

"Yah. You gotta get us back to San Dimas. Beam us up or something," added Ted.

"You must play me again," the Grim Reaper said with an evil smile.

"What?" yelled Bill. "That's not fair. We had a deal. One game, one shot. That's what you said, dude."

"Best two out of three," said the Reaper with an evil smile.

"No way!" yelped Ted. "If we had lost, would

you have given *us* another chance? I don't think so."

"I'm telling you, this is not playing fair. You can't change the rules just because you lost."

"Yah!" Ted agreed.

The Grim Reaper shrugged. "No one ever said Death was fair, sonny."

"We had a deal!" Ted was totally outraged.

The Grim Reaper poked him in the chest with his bony index finger. "Look, kid, this is the underworld. I'm Death. Who do you think makes the rules around here? *Me*, that's who."

They couldn't really think of a way to argue with that. Death was, after all, a pretty slippery character.

The next game was just as tense as Battleship, and again the Grim Reaper considered himself a master of the situation. After hours of nail-biting play, the Grim Reaper was confident, poised and ready to deliver the fatal blow.

"I believe: Colonel Mustard did it. In the study. With . . . the candlestick."

Bill and Ted exhaled heavily, relieved. "Sorry, Death, you lose. Totally."

"Yah. That's two out of two, Death-dude."

"Now can we go back?"

"Best three out of five!" Death snapped.

"Aww, dude, you promised."

"I lied," said Death.

"I just don't believe this guy," said Ted.

"Yah. If you can't trust Death, who can you trust?"

Death was getting panicky now—he had to win *something* against these two dudes. But he made a bad choice of game, choosing to challenge Bill and Ted to an old game of electric football—a game that was almost impossible to play, never mind win.

It was a rout from the beginning. Death couldn't get his rushers to rush, his quarterback couldn't pass, his blockers couldn't block.

"Face it, dude, you most heinously lost this game," said Ted.

"Hit the shower, Grim Reaper."

Death looked so furious his eyes seem to glow. In a single wild blow, he swept his players from the board. The little men went scattering all over the place.

Bill rolled his eyes. "Best of seven, right?"

"Right!" snarled the Grim Reaper.

You would have thought that Twister would be the Grim Reaper's game, him being so tall and everything, but the dude was so uncoordinated that it was a wonder he could walk down the street.

Bill and Death were intertwined on the Twister mat, and already it looked bad for Death. Ted spun the spinner and gave Bill his instructions.

"Right hand . . . blue." Bill placed his hand

where it was supposed to be with ease.

Death was breathing hard.

"Okay, Grim Reaper," said Ted. "Left foot . . . green."

Death gritted his teeth and tried to stretch for the designated spot. No luck—sweating and swearing, he fell on his butt.

By now, Bill and Ted were used to winning and getting nothing for it, so they more or less expected the Grim Reaper to suggest a game of checkers or Parcheesi, but they were surprised. Death didn't want to play any more. He was tired, for one thing, and he had a sneaking feeling that he wouldn't be able to win at anything he played with Bill and Ted, and it was humiliating to lose time and again like that.

"I will—" It almost hurt physically to say these hated words. "I will take you back."

Bill and Ted sighed in relief. Ted reached down—no hard feelings—and helped the Grim Reaper to his feet.

"Death, I gotta say, you played very well."

"Don't patronize me, kid," snapped Death. His pride had already been bruised enough for one day.

"Sorry, dude."

"You know, you got a lot to learn about sportsmanship," observed Bill.

Death was in no mood to be lectured by Bill or Ted on anything, leave alone the ethics of winning and losing. Death had never lost before and he didn't like the feeling. It was best to get his humiliation over and done with.

"This way," he said shortly, leading them from the game chamber.

Bill and Ted followed, grateful that their ordeal was over and that they could get back to the business at hand.

"Now we can go back and save the babes."

"Yah . . ." Ted's brow furrowed. "But you know, Bill, when we get back, how're we gonna fight those other us's, those robot dudes? They're way stronger than us and they're way smarter than us . . ."

Bill nodded. "Plus they've already killed us once already, don't forget. That's got to give them momentum."

"Okay, if we were good human us's . . ."

"Which, if you think about it, we are . . ."

"Right. If we were us and we needed to figure out a way to fight two robot us's, what would we do?"

"Most tough, dude."

They pondered on this problem for a moment; then Ted had an idea. "Wait! They've got bad robot us's . . ."

"Yah?"

"So what do you need to fight bad robot us's?"

"*Good* robot us's?" said Bill uncertainly.

"Makes sense, doesn't it?"

Bill was jubilant. "Ted, that's it. Totally good thinking, dude!"

Ted's elation didn't last long, though. "Only how are we going to build 'em?"

Bill pointed to the Grim Reaper. "How about him? Maybe he knows."

"I don't think building good robots is exactly his line, dude."

"Doesn't hurt to ask." He tapped the Grim Reaper on the shoulder. "Excuse us, Death, but before we go back, could you take us to someone who can help us?"

Death sighed. If they hadn't asked, he wouldn't have had to tell them the consequences of their having vanquished him in so many games.

"You have beaten me," he said in a resigned, tired voice. "I am now yours to command. If you need help, I must provide it."

"Excellent!" they said.

"Follow me . . ." The Grim Reaper led the way.

Bill nodded, as if everything made sense now. "Dude . . ."

"What?"

"Don't Fear the Reaper."

"Totally true, dude."

They air-guitared quietly, aware that a universal truth had been revealed to them, via the underworld and Blue Oyster Cult.

Chapter
7

Bill and Ted weren't the best housekeepers in the world. Evil Bill and Evil Ted were even worse—horrible, in fact. They were also totally into mindless destruction, and while Good Bill and Good Ted had their faults, destroying for destroying's sake was not one of them. Of course, they knew that once they got the Wyld Stallyns off the ground, they would have to destroy a few thousand dollars' worth of equipment whenever they played some live gigs in mega-arenas—the fans would expect it—but that was in the future, when they could afford it.

With Evil Bill and Evil Ted, on the other hand, it was not only their life's work, what they had been totally programmed to do, but it was their hobby as well. Now, having destroyed the relationship between Good Ted and Good Bill and the princesses and murdering Bill and Ted into the bargain, Evil Bill and Evil Ted were addressing themselves to the question of trashing Bill and Ted's apartment. They were very good at it. Pros, you might say.

They had already had a certain amount of fun tearing up what there was of Bill and Ted's meager wardrobe, flushing smaller household items down the toilet and totally scratching and smashing their prized collection of Aerosmith and Iron Maiden records. The stereo and the TV were just smoking shells, the posters had been stripped from the walls, the rug ripped up from the floor, the curtains destroyed, the furniture hacked to splinters.

Evil Bill and Evil Ted now turned to the kitchen and found that that was a very entertaining venue, opening up many opportunities for creative and imaginative ways of destroying things.

Ted threw open the door of the refrigerator and yanked out a can of soda. He shook it furiously and then fired a long stream of sticky liquid at Evil Bill.

"You look thirsty, dude!" cackled Evil Ted.

"And you look hungry!" yelled Evil Bill. He grabbed a handful of eggs from the rack in the door of the refrigerator and pasted Evil Ted in the side of the head with two of them.

"Yah!" Evil Ted squeezed some of the yolk

from his hair. "And I know what you want!"

"What?"

"Dessert, dude!" Evil Ted pulled out an aerosol can of whipped cream topping and blasted away at Evil Bill. Cream, eggs and soda made the kitchen floor sticky underfoot, and just for the heck of it, Evil Bill and Evil Ted pulled all the food out of the refrigerator, tossed it to the ground and trampled it into paste.

Then they turned their attention to the kitchen cabinets, inventing, on the spur of the moment, a new kind of basketball. Instead of using a ball, like normal people, or even normal robots, they played with all the glassware—plates, glasses, saucers—that they found in the cabinets. True, you couldn't dribble a plate—no bounce, right?—but it did make for a very satisfying slam dunk.

You see, Bill and Ted had a little indoor basketball net over their kitchen door, and sometimes, when they had to have some very serious and deep conversation, they would sit at their kitchen counter, talking about the Wyld Stallyns, their babes, their future and other serious things, shooting a nerf ball at the hoop. It helped them concentrate and it didn't do any harm.

That just wasn't Evil Bill and Evil Ted's kind of game. Evil Ted had a big water glass in his right hand, and he was backing in toward the basket, his left arm out to keep Evil Bill out of the way. Evil Bill, for his part, was working hard to block, in Evil Ted's face, trying to prevent the attacker from getting a look at the basket.

"No way, dude," said Evil Bill, "you'll never get through my totally non-heinous and most resplendent blocking."

"Yah?" Evil Ted powered in a few feet and hooked the glass at the basket. It sailed through the air, end over end, whiffed through the basket and exploded with a crash on the tile floor.

"Two points, dude!"

"Lucky, dude, that's all. My turn." He scooped up a dinner plate, faked right, went left and blew by Evil Ted, leaped for the hoop and jammed, slamming the plate to smithereens.

"He shoots! He scores!" yelled Evil Bill. "The man, er, robot is unstoppable!"

Evil Ted had an armful of glasses, and he was standing about where he imagined the free throw line to be, pitching them toward the basket. Not all of them swished—a couple of them just smashed against the kitchen wall, showering glass over everything—but most found their target and then shattered.

Evil Bill did his best to help out, goaltending, tipping in a few of the rim shots. It sounded as if it were raining broken glass in the wreckage of Bill and Ted's apartment.

Then, abruptly, it stopped.

"More!" demanded Evil Bill.

Evil Ted was peering into the cupboards,

rummaging around, throwing out cans and cereal boxes, rifling the shelves, like a thief searching for hidden valuables.

"Bad news, dude."

"What?"

"Game's over. We are totally out of dishes!"

"Heinous."

They looked for a moment over the extensive wreckage, smiles of satisfaction on their faces.

"Well," said Evil Bill. "It was fun while it lasted. I just wish those other us's had more stuff to wreck."

"Well, we didn't make all that much at Pretzels 'n' Cheese, dude."

"Yah, but I wish we had spent more on decorating."

Evil Ted suddenly had a totally triumphant idea. "Wait, Evil Bill, check this out."

"What?"

"This, dude." Evil Ted put his hands around his neck, as if he were trying to strangle himself, and pulled. His electronic, completely solid-state head popped out of his neck, trailing a few wires like tentacles. His headless body thundered across the kitchen, crunching glass underfoot, and slam-dunked his own indestructible head into the basket.

"Two points!" Evil Ted's head roared as it rolled across the kitchen floor.

Evil Bill was most impressed with this new variation on the game. True, they were trashing themselves now, but trashing is trashing.

"Not bad, dude, not bad."

"That's what I call heads-up basketball, dude." Evil Ted's head was still on the floor, and it was giving a certain amount of thought to the problem of how to get back to his body.

"Here," said Evil Bill, "lemme try that." Just as Evil Ted had done, Evil Bill pulled his head off his neck, as easily as popping a tab on a soft-drink can. "Check this out, Evil Ted. Keep your eye on the ball and watch a perfect Kareem-style sky hook." Evil Bill lofted his own head high in the air, a long graceful arc that seemed to be perfectly on target—until it slammed into one of the blades of the ceiling fan in the kitchen. It stuck there and turned slowly around, as if it were on a merry-go-round.

"Whoaaaaaa!" shouted Evil Bill's head. "Totally bogus!"

"Dude! You totally didn't see the fan!" Evil Ted's body, all on its own, decided it was time it had a head back. It reached down and grabbed it and stuffed it back on his neck.

Evil Bill's head continued to turn round and round. It was beginning to make him a little dizzy.

"Evil Ted! Get my body to get over here and take me off this thing."

"Yah! You heard him, dude," said the now-complete Evil Ted to Evil Bill's headless torso. "Go get your head, dude."

Instead of doing what it was told, the body casually waved to Evil Bill's twirling head, gesturing to him as if it didn't give a damn whether it ever got back with its head again.

"Whoooaaa!" said Evil Ted. "What a lousy attitude you have, Evil Bill."

"As soon as I get back to my body, dude, I am gonna totally beat myself black and blue."

"You'll totally have it coming to you, Evil Bill. Trouble is it's gonna hurt you more than it'll hurt yourself."

"It'll be worth it. Evil Ted, dude, get me down from here, would ya please?"

"Yah!" Evil Ted leaped as if going up for a jump shot, grabbed the head off the fan blade and came down lightly. This seemed to get Evil Bill's body's attention. Evil Ted waved the head at the body. "Got your head, dude!" he said tauntingly.

"Stop fooling around, Evil Ted, and totally reunite me with my body."

"No way, dude!" Evil Ted tucked the head into the crook of his right arm like a football running back. "I'm gonna score a touchdown!"

Evil Bill's voice was muffled. "Gotta get through my triumphant defense first." Evil Bill's headless body charged toward Evil Ted like a tough front-line blocker. "I'm gonna totally tackle you, dude!"

"No way!" Evil Ted danced around Evil Bill's body, raced into the living room and spiked Evil Bill's head into a wastebasket. "Touchdown for Evil Ted! Now for the triumphant field goal!"

"You're not kicking my head anywhere, dude!" Evil Bill's body rushed into the living room and grabbed the head out of the wastebasket. Quickly he jammed the head back on his shoulders. "That's better."

"That was fun!" said Evil Ted.

"Yah! Way to go, dude! We are truly most resplendent total headbangers."

"Yah!" Evil Ted air-guitared wildly for a moment, then stopped stock-still, a funny look on his face.

"What's up, Evil Ted?"

"We're wanted on the phone, Evil Bill. It's the boss from head office." Evil Ted smacked the back of his head and his eye popped into his hand. There was a moment of static and fuzz in the pupil, then De Nomolos's sneery face came on the screen.

"How's it goin', master-dude?"

De Nomolos looked with utter contempt at his two evil creations. Even though they were central to his plan, he couldn't help but loathe these two creatures. He looked forward to a time when not only would there be no Bill and Ted, but no manmade Bill and Teds either. Bliss . . .

"Give me a report," snapped De Nomolos. "At once!"

"We totally ruined things between Joanna and Elizabeth and Bill and Ted," said Evil Bill.

"Yah. They were most sad dudes when we totally murdered them."

"Yah! And now we've been having a little R and R while we trash their heinous apartment."

"Stop wasting time," De Nomolos barked. "You must proceed with the plan. Immediately, do you understand me?"

"Yes, master-dude!" they said in unison.

"Understand me, you cretins," said De Nomolos, "it is not enough that you destroy those two . . . those two . . . ," he couldn't even bring himself to say their names, " . . . imbeciles. It is imperative that you destroy everything about them."

"Totally!" agreed Evil Bill and Evil Ted.

"So get on with it," De Nomolos ordered. "Follow your orders to the letter."

"Okay, dude," said Evil Ted. "What's next? What does the program say?"

"Don't think! You're not programmed to think!" yelled De Nomolos. "Just do! The next phase consists of completely alienating Bill and Ted from everyone they've ever known."

"Right!" said Evil Bill.

"Excellent!" said Evil Ted. "You are one most smart dude, dude."

De Nomolos looked with disgust at the machines he had created in the image of his greatest enemies. "I hate them and I hate robot versions of them."

"Hey, dude," said Evil Bill, "don't blame us. You're the one who made us."

"Yah!" said Evil Ted.

"Don't remind me," said De Nomolos. "Get to work!"

The image on the eye monitor fuzzed over and De Nomolos disappeared. Back in the future, he was busy implementing his own part in the plan, which consisted mainly of indoctrinating his captive students at Bill and Ted University in the history he had so carefully and nastily rewritten.

"Pop quiz!" he said suddenly to the class. "Close your books!"

Thomas Edison, Bach and the rest of the class closed their personal copies of a not very fascinating book called *Nomolos de Nomolos—The Greatest Man in History* and sat up straight.

De Nomolos scowled at the ranks of students. "In what year did Robot Ted marry Missy?" He scanned the room, as if about to choose a candidate for execution. "Thomas Edison! Answer me!"

Edison started as if he had been pinched and swallowed hard. It had been a while since he had taken a pop quiz, and he had never taken one with a gun to his head. It was a most disconcerting feeling.

"Uh . . . 1996?" he asked hopefully.

De Nomolos actually smiled, an expression that looked sort of peculiar, out of place on his face. "Very good. You are as smart as your reputation said you were."

Seeing as Edison was on De Nomolos's good side, he thought he might use the opportunity to get out of the jam he found himself in. "Sir, I hate to bother you, but I have to be getting back to New Jersey to invent the motion picture, and I happen to know that Johann Sebastian Bach here was halfway through *Das Musicalishes Opfer*—really smoking, really on a roll too—so maybe we could be heading back to our own times now."

Edison wasn't teacher's pet anymore. "Shut up. You know no one can leave the century during a quiz. Leads to cheating. Now . . . you!" He pointed to a student in the third row who was so scared she jumped about a foot in the air.

"Me?"

"Yes, you . . ." De Nomolos's brow furrowed as if he was trying to think up a real toughie. "In what year did Missy marry Robot Bill?"

"1998," she said quickly.

De Nomolos smiled his bad guy smile. "Good . . . Good . . . Things are coming along very nicely, very nicely indeed." De Nomolos looked around the room, drawing a bead on another hapless student, like a sniper fixing a victim in the cross hairs of his sights. "You! All the time that Robot Bill and Robot Ted were on earth, where were the actual Bill and Ted?"

The student swallowed hard. "They were dead, sir. Totally."

"*Exactly*." De Nomolos spoke with a great and obvious sense of satisfaction. Things seemed to be going his way, just as planned. "Gone . . . dead. Never to return again. And that means that their idiocy will have died with them. No one can do anything about it. Ingenious, isn't it?"

Well, Bill and Ted may have been in Hell, but dead they certainly weren't. Having beaten the Grim Reaper at—well, they couldn't really call it his own game—having beaten the Reaper, they weren't sure just what it was they were supposed to do next. Even with the Grim Reaper on your side, figuring out a way to build good robot versions of yourself is not exactly something that most people—never mind Bill and Ted—would find all that easy.

However, Death seemed to have a pretty fair idea of what was going on—at least he seemed to know where he was going, a claim that Bill and Ted would have been hard pressed to make.

They were in a fairly quiet part of the nether regions, and they seemed to be headed slowly but surely uphill. Death was trudging along, just ahead of Bill and Ted, not standoffish, exactly, but they definitely got the feeling that he was still a little embarrassed by having been beaten so badly by them. It seemed, also, as if he wasn't crazy about being seen with Bill and Ted, not just yet, anyway. Maybe, they thought, he'd warm up a little when he got to know them better.

The funny thing was, the weather, or, more accurately, the atmosphere, the *ambience* was changing. It was cooler and quieter now. Bill and Ted felt better too. Admittedly, anything would be better than the underworld, but things just seemed a little calmer, which was good, considering all they had been through recently.

Still, it wasn't like they weren't anxious to get back to San Dimas and to save the princesses from the attentions of Evil Bill and Evil Ted— a fate Good Bill and Good Ted could now safely say, from experience, was worse than death. Far worse.

"Excuse me, Grim Reaper," asked Bill. "But do you think you could, like, tell us where we're going, dude?"

Death stretched out a long bony arm and pointed. They were approaching the entrance to a place that could only be described as serene. Things were changing too—the decor had gone from being a neutral kind of beige color to a very enlightened-looking lavender-and-white. There were other people on the path too, walking dreamily past Bill and Ted and the Grim Reaper. They were all different—there was a big dude in a full football uniform, pads, helmet, the works; an Indian woman in a sari; a woman who looked like she'd just stepped off a tennis court someplace (she still carried her racket); even a totally non-heinous babe in a bathing suit—except for one thing that Bill and Ted noticed immediately. Their clothing, different though it may have been, all conformed to the lavender-and-white color scheme: the football uniform, the tennis clothes, the sari, the bathing suit, all looked as if they had come from the same place.

Bill, Ted and the Grim Reaper were not dressed in lavender and white. It made Bill and Ted feel self-conscious, as if they had shown up at a formal party dressed for the beach. It also tended to make them stand out from the crowd.

"Whoa . . . this is most atypical," said Ted.

"This way," said the Grim Reaper. His voice was still creepy, and Bill and Ted got the feeling that he felt they didn't belong there.

Standing just inside the entrance were several men and women, their faces glowing with happiness and serenity, as if they knew not just some, but *all* of the universal truths and didn't have a care in the world. Or maybe it was just that they had had a good night's sleep.

One of the women stepped forward and started handing out parchment scrolls to the new arrivals. She handed one to Ted too. "Welcome," she said in a soft, musical voice. "Welcome to Eternity."

Ted smiled pleasantly. "Hello." He took the scroll but wasn't sure what he was supposed to do with it. He had never figured himself to be the scroll-reading type. "Thanks," he said, "thanks a lot."

Bill was looking around with great interest. "So this is Eternity. Nice."

The Grim Reaper stood off to one side looking bored. Maybe he didn't belong in Eternity, but it wasn't like this was his first trip. Ted was busy studying the scroll.

" 'Only the most serene and enlightened souls shall gain audience.' Bill, dude, these people seem pretty easygoing, but I have a feeling this serene enlightenment stuff is something they take most seriously. It's like a house rule."

"Serene and enlightened souls . . . ," said Bill. "Dude, we're in big trouble."

"Yah. We *have* to get in. Otherwise the Grim Reaper wouldn't have bothered to bring us here."

Bill peered longingly through Heaven's gate. "We have to think of something, dude."

"Hey, Grim Reaper, if we get in, all our troubles could be solved, right?"

The Grim Reaper whistled and studied his cracked and split old fingernails. "Maybe . . . ," he said.

"So help us, dude," said Ted.

"Can't," said the Grim Reaper.

"Wait," said Bill, "you said you *had* to help us if we beat you at all those games."

"Help you as much as I can," said the Grim Reaper. "Heaven, you understand, just isn't my turf." He smiled evilly and then added, "Dudes."

"But," countered Ted, "if we do get in, you can keep on helping us, right?"

"Right."

"I got an idea," said Bill.

Bill and Ted went into a huddle and consulted briefly. Ted felt nervous about Bill's plan, but he couldn't see any other way out of their predicament.

"It's your idea, dude," Ted told Bill. "*You* do it. And Grim Reaper . . ."

The figure of Death pointed his scythe at himself. "Who? Me?"

"Yeah, you. You're in on this too, dude."

"No way."

"Yes way. You have to help us. It's part of the deal."

The Grim Reaper's thin shoulders slumped and he shuffled over to Bill and Ted. "The things I get myself into," he muttered.

The three of them walked up to the men and women still standing at the gates of Heaven and smiled pleasantly. They looked so serene and enlightened that Bill and Ted felt totally bogus about what they were going to do. The Grim Reaper didn't look all that happy about it either.

"Do it, Bill," said Ted.

"Okay . . ." Bill swallowed deeply. "Excuse us, wise dudes, but, uh, could we ask you a question?"

"Do you seek enlightenment?" asked one of the men.

"Or serenity?" said the woman who had handed Ted the scroll.

"Well . . . ," said Bill, "neither, really, not exactly . . ."

"Neither?" said the other gatekeeper.

"Go ahead, dude," said Ted, urging Bill on.

"I can't," said Bill. "Grim Reaper, you do it."

"What . . . uh, what we wanted to ask you was . . ."

Ted found his voice and thought of the most serene question he could summon up. "Yah. Okay. What is more beautiful, the song of the nightingale or just after?"

"I beg your pardon?" said one of the serene dudes.

"Just before, maybe?" suggested the Grim Reaper.

"Whoaa!" Bill shouted unexpectedly. "Look, dudes! It's Elvis!"

The three serene people turned to catch sight of the King, and that was all the time Bill, Ted and the Grim Reaper needed to get what they wanted. They fell on the three gatekeepers and in a matter of seconds had administered a lightning-quick series of melvins followed by the first petty thefts ever committed in the precincts beyond the pearly gates.

The enlightened and serene citizens of Heaven never knew what hit them. One minute they were pondering a serene and enlightened—if obscure—question from some admittedly rather peculiar people. The next thing they knew, they were flat on their backs, their robes gone.

Bill, Ted and the Grim Reaper were dashing

through Heaven, busily pulling on the robes they had stolen.

"Dude, we're in heaven and we just mugged three people," said Ted, aghast at what they had actually done and where they had done it.

"Yah," said Bill, equally shocked at their behavior. "We better get outta here before we ruin it for everybody." He shot a glance over his shoulder at the Grim Reaper. "C'mon, dude, let's move it."

"I can't wear this!" grumbled the Grim Reaper. He had gotten the robes that had belonged to the woman. They had a definitely feminine look about them. Bill and Ted's garments didn't look exactly normal either, but at least they had gotten clothing more suitable for guys.

Despite their predicament, Bill and Ted couldn't help but laugh at the Grim Reaper's discomfort.

"You look great, dude," said Ted, stifling a laugh as the Grim Reaper shimmied into the woman's clothing.

"Yah," said Bill with a laugh, "you do. Totally. I mean, Grim Reaper, it's *you*."

"Oh, shut up," snapped the Grim Reaper. "You still need me, you know. You wouldn't get ten feet without me."

Ted was still smirking. The Grim Reaper in women's clothing was not something you see every day, and Ted had to admit, as babes went, Death looked most non-triumphant. Totally.

But both Bill and Ted realized that there was an element of truth in what the Grim Reaper said. If it hadn't been for Death, in fact, they would still be dead. It was a lucky break for them running into him.

"Yah," said Bill, "what do we do next?"

"There's another gate," said the Grim Reaper. "That's the tough one."

"What was the last one?" asked Ted, suddenly worried. "I mean, I thought we were in."

"That was reception," said the Grim Reaper. "The next one is security."

"Bogus," said Bill. "Do you think we'll pass? I mean, we are dressed like serene, enlightened and wise dudes, right?"

The Grim Reaper shook his head. "Not good enough. Looking the part is one thing. *Acting* the part—that's something else."

"So what do we do?" asked Ted.

The Grim Reaper shrugged. "Like I have all the answers?"

"It's simple, Ted. Just act wise."

"Act wise?" said Ted dubiously. That was some tall order.

"Yah, like this . . ." Bill did his best to assume what he thought might be a look of great wisdom, enlightenment and serenity. He tried to look solemn and at the same time get a faraway look in his eyes, as if the music of the celestial spheres were forever playing in his brain.

"Nice try," said Ted.

"Don't I look wise?"

"Well . . . wiser." Ted composed his face in much the same manner. "How about me?"

"Close enough," said Bill. "Grim Reaper, how about you? How's your wise look?"

"Listen," hissed the Grim Reaper, pulling the collar of his robe up to hide as much of his face as he could. "I don't want the gatekeeper to see me at all."

"Why not?" asked Bill.

" 'Cause I'm not supposed to be here. I mean, the Grim Reaper in Heaven? I'd kinda stand out like a sore thumb, wouldn't you say?"

"Don't worry about a thing, Death-dude," said Ted reassuringly. "No one is going to expect the Grim Reaper to show up dressed like a babe."

"Yah. Just act the part," said Bill.

"And let us do all the talking," said Ted.

"Oh, great," said the Grim Reaper.

The official keeper of the gates of Heaven was as serene and enlightened as the people at reception, but he looked a little suspicious too when Bill, Ted and the Grim Reaper presented themselves for admittance.

"How's it going?" asked Bill in his best wise voice. "I am, uh, William, uh, William the Wyld."

"And I am uh . . . Ted the Stallyn."

"Welcome," said the gatekeeper. He looked at the Grim Reaper, raising an eyebrow as he did so. Death coughed nervously and rubbed the place on his skull where his eyebrows would have been if he had had any.

"And you are . . . ?" asked the gatekeeper.

"This is our girlfriend," said Bill quickly. "Her name is, uh . . ."

"Death," said Ted.

"Deathina," corrected Bill instantly.

The gatekeeper's eyes narrowed and he stared intently at the Grim Reaper. "You seem so familiar. I'm sure we've met before. Don't I know you?"

The Grim Reaper hauled his deep voice out of a bass pit and tried his best at a babe-like falsetto. "Nooo," he trilled. He sounded pretty ridiculous.

The gatekeeper stared at him a moment longer and then shrugged. This was Heaven after all, where lying was not exactly common, so if the Grim Reaper said they had not met before, the chances were good he was telling the truth.

"Do you wish to enter?" asked the gate-keeper.

"Totally," said Ted.

"Then you must answer a single question." The gatekeeper unrolled a scroll and read from it. "What," he asked, "is the meaning of life?"

Bill and Ted winced. That was a little harder than they had expected.

"The meaning of life . . . ," said Bill. The meaning of life, he thought, was babes and bands, but he was pretty sure that was not the answer the gatekeeper of Heaven had in mind. "The meaning of life . . . well, see . . . Okay. That's like a two-part answer, and to answer the first part, please welcome warmly, Ted the Stallyn . . . Ted? The meaning of life, if you please."

"Yah. The meaning of life. Right. Okay." He closed his eyes tight and hoped for inspiration. He must have been doing something right because he got some. "The meaning of life: 'Every rose has its thorn. Just like every night has its dawn.' Take it, Bill the Wyld . . ."

"Okay . . . 'Just like every cowboy sings a sad, sad song . . . ' Deathina?"

" 'Every rose has its thorn,' " said Deathina. "That's it. Okay?"

The gatekeeper paused a moment. It wasn't the usual answer, but he figured if he graded on a curve, they were in. "Very well," he said, "you may enter."

"Excellent!" said Bill, Ted and the Grim Reaper.

The Grim Reaper led them away from the gates and into Heaven proper. Just as before, he seemed to know where he was headed, even if, technically, he didn't really belong there. They were following a wide path that ran from the gate deep into the peaceful kingdom, toward a bright white light that seemed at once far off and then, all of a sudden, close at hand. It was weird, but given the experiences Bill and Ted had been having in the last few days, the weird was beginning to become quite commonplace. It was amazing how you could get used to anything after a while.

"So?" asked Ted. "Now what?"

The Grim Reaper pointed toward the light. Emanating from it was a staircase, leading up into the cloud of blinding white, shimmering light.

"We go up there?" asked Bill, looking up into the glowing cloud.

"Don't be ridiculous," said the Grim Reaper, rolling his eyes. "No one goes up there—just . . . Him."

"Whoaaa . . . ," said Bill and Ted, overcome with awe.

"How do we talk to . . . Him?" asked Bill.

"With total respect, dude," said Ted soberly.

"And tell the truth," said the Grim Reaper.

Bill stopped at the base of the stairs and stared into the white light. The Grim Reaper's advice seemed good, so he decided to start with the truth. "Okay. God. As if you didn't know already, we're not the three wise people you might think that we are."

Ted shook his head. "No, you see, we mugged some guys and took their clothes. Sorry. Really."

They felt better for having gotten that confession out of the way, and He seemed to be taking it pretty well, which was decent.

"Anyways," said Bill, brightening, "I'm Bill S. Preston, Esquire."

"And I'm Ted 'Theodore' Logan."

"And together," they said, "we are . . . Wyld Stallyns."

If they expected applause or even simple recognition, they were disappointed.

"Yah," said Bill, pressing along gamely. "And this lovely lady is the Grim Reaper. He brought us here when we challenged him to a whole bunch of different games and we won them all."

"Totally," said Ted emphatically.

The Grim Reaper really wished they hadn't brought that up. Embarrassed, he half waved, glanced into the brightness and then looked down at the ground, feeling his humiliation acutely. It was bad enough being embarrassed in the underworld, but now everybody in Heaven was going to hear about it as well. He wouldn't be able to show his face for at least half an aeon.

Bill and Ted were unaware of the Grim Reaper's discomfort. They had their own problems, and now they were on the verge of getting around to solving them.

"Now," said Ted. "Okay. First of all, congratulations on Earth. It is a most excellent planet, and I have to say that Bill and I enjoy it on a daily basis."

Bill nodded in agreement. "And we should

mention your other excellent achievements, the other planets."

"Yah," said Ted enthusiastically. "Like, uh, Mars . . . Jupiter . . . Pluto . . ."

"Uranus," Bill added.

The Grim Reaper rolled his eyes. "Stop wasting his time, guys, he's busy."

"Oh. Yah. Right," said Ted.

"The point is," said Bill, "it is most non-triumphant. The point is this. Okay. We died."

"Most unfairly," said Ted, not a little aggrieved.

"But," said Bill, pressing on, "we won the chance to go back. And now we want to construct something to help save the women we love."

"Yah," said Ted, "and we really don't got all that much time.

"So we were wondering . . ." Bill really hated asking for favors, but it had to be done. "We were wondering . . . Do you think maybe you could help us to find, like, the greatest scientist in the universe? If it's not too much trouble."

"Right," said Ted, "if it's an inconvenience, forget we ever asked."

There was a pause from on high, and for one very uncomfortable moment, Bill, Ted and the Grim Reaper thought they just might have caught God at a bad moment—and that meant that Bill and Ted would never get back to San Dimas and save the princesses from Evil Bill and Evil Ted. For the second time that day their fates hung in the balance. They had a feeling that it was not worth their while to challenge God to a game of Twister either. They would lose that one.

But then, floating slowly down from the bright cloud of light, came a shimmering piece of parchment. Bill reached up, grabbed it and studied the single word inscribed on it.

"What's it say, dude?" asked Ted.

"It says 'Station.'"

"Whoa . . . ," said Ted, not quite sure what his reaction should be.

Together he and Bill looked into the light. "Thanks," they said, "we really appreciate it. Whatever it means . . ."

"We have to say," said Bill, "that you are a most just and noble Creator."

"Yah," said Ted. "Totally. And we have taken up enough of your most valuable time."

"Okay." Bill waved into the light. "Well, we'll be going now."

"Yah," said Ted. "Keep up the good work."

"Catch you later, God!"

The Grim Reaper started to usher them off the platform, but suddenly Ted stopped. He figured as long as he was here he might as well get the answer to something that had been bothering him for at least a week.

"Oh. There's just one thing I always wondered and maybe you can clear it up for me. Who shot JR? You know, JR? The most mean dude on 'Dallas.'"

Bill yanked Ted away by the collar of his serene and enlightened costume. "Dude—that was ten years ago!"

Ted looked extremely puzzled. "It was? But I just saw it on channel ten."

"Rerun, dude."

"Oh. Well, who *did* shoot JR?"

"I'll tell you later."

"Okay." Ted waved good-bye yet again. "Well, that's it, I guess. See ya, dude."

But it wasn't quite it. The Grim Reaper really felt the need to explain his own sorry state of affairs. He looked into the light.

"Sorry," he said. "But, you see, they melvined me." He shrugged ruefully. "What could I do?"

He knew it wasn't much of an excuse, but it was the best he could think of on the spur of the moment.

Chapter
8

Heaven, it turned out, was quite an interesting place, once you got to know your way around, and the people looked pretty resplendent too. Bill and Ted, with their newfound interest in history, were totally amazed to see so many people they recognized. It also seemed that in Heaven you could pretty much hang out with whomever you wanted. Like, when they saw Thomas Jefferson tossing a frisbee, they were pretty sure that it would be George Washington or maybe Ben Franklin catching it, but it turned out to be Shakespeare who was throwing it back.

There were also a lot of people they didn't recognize, but Bill and Ted figured they were just ordinary people who had spent their lives getting as serene and as enlightened as it took to get past the gatekeeper.

Bill, Ted and the Grim Reaper didn't feel so much like frauds now—they had taken off their wise people clothes—and while they didn't exactly blend in, no one gave them a second glance. It must have gotten around that it was okay for them to be there.

Bill was studying the map they had received closely, but he was still puzzled. "Well, I think we're in the right place," he said, scratching his head. "Now alls we got to do is find this scientist."

"What kind of name is Station anyway?"

"Must be from the future or something," said Bill, "but I have to admit that it is a most confusing name. And how are we supposed to know the dude when we find him? Grim Reaper, do you know this Station-dude?"

The Grim Reaper got all coy and superior-looking. "Maybe," he said with a smirk. "Maybe not."

"Yeah, well thanks, dude," said Bill, rolling his eyes in disgust. Then his eyes lit up—he recognized someone, having seen his face on numerous posters and T-shirts. "Ted, check it out."

"What?"

"Him," said Bill, pointing at an elderly man who was strolling through Heaven deep in conversation with an Oriental dude. The man had a deeply lined face and a great mane of white hair.

Ted knew him instantly. "Whoaa . . . Albert Einstein."

The great German scientist was kind of a hero to Bill and Ted because Einstein had formulated a theory, the Theory of Relativity, concerning time, space and the motion of objects. Now, normally, such deep subjects would not be of much interest to Bill and Ted, but Einstein's theory of relativity proved that time travel was possible—theoretically. In their case, however, they *had* traveled through time, space being the Circuits of Time and the objects being Bill and Ted. Einstein was to time travel what big hair and guitars are to heavy metal. In short, the Eddie Van Halen of science.

Bill marched right up to their idol. "Excuse me, Albert Einstein, I'm Bill S. Preston, Esquire . . ."

"And I'm Ted 'Theodore' Logan."

"How do you do," said the scientist politely. "May I present my good friend, Confucius." He gestured toward his companion, who bowed from the waist.

"Whoa," said Ted, "you're the dude who writes all those cookies."

"The Analects," said Confucius.

"Whatever," said Ted.

"Al," said Bill, "if you had to name the greatest scientist in the universe—excluding yourself, of course—who would that dude be?"

"Well," said Einstein, "that's easy. There's

one far greater than I *ever* was. His name is Station."

Bill and Ted looked at each other and grinned and air-guitared briefly.

"And where can we find him, dude?" asked Ted.

"I believe I saw him over there." Einstein pointed a few yards away to a little gazebo.

"Thanks, Albert Einstein," said Ted. "By the way, we enjoyed your theory of relativity."

"Yah," said Bill, "but we must tell you—not only is time travel possible, but it is also a most enjoyable experience and must be experienced at every opportunity."

"Oh, that is good to know," said Einstein.

"C'mon," said the Grim Reaper, "let's get this show on the road."

When you conjure up a mental image of a scientist, you're likely to think of a serious-looking, quiet dude like Einstein, or, at least, of some nerdy guy in a white lab coat with a plastic pocket protector and a very complicated calculator on his belt, right? Not Station. The first time Bill and Ted saw him, they were not impressed—you see, even if a scientist doesn't look like you imagine a scientist to look, you at least expect him to be *human*—that's not too much to ask. Definitely not Station.

First of all, there were two of them, and as best as Bill and Ted could figure out, together the two of them added up to Station. They were also not the handsomest guys either, but they had been vouched for by Albert Einstein *and* God, so Bill and Ted had really good reasons for believing they were the best.

But they were most odd looking. Totally.

The Stations were gnomelike little guys, cute in a troll kind of way. Short with lumpy bodies, long arms and big butts, they had these little tufts of hair on their heads. They had friendly expressions on their funny faces, the most dominant feature being their long, snoutlike nose. They were a nice shade of rust, or maybe terra-cotta, as if they spent a lot of time at the beach or on a tanning bed on Mars or wherever they were from. One thing for sure—they weren't human.

Okay. They didn't look like scientists, but more disconcerting, they didn't *act* like scientists either. Scientists are supposed to stand around doing scientific things like experiments, or at least talking about heavy science stuff. Not Station.

The two little lumpy dudes with the big butts were standing in a small glade in a quiet corner of Heaven, and they seemed to be playing.

"Mr. Station . . . ," began Bill, "we are in a most heinous situation which—"

"Staaaaaaation," said one of the little creatures in a high-pitched nasally kind of voice.

"Huh?" said Bill.

"Station," replied the other dude.

That seemed to be a signal of some kind—

at least, it made sense to the Station—because right at that moment the two creatures began running in a little circle, then—this was weird, even to Bill and Ted, who had a high weirdness threshold—one of them jumped high in the air, did a somersault and landed bang on top of his head. His companion clapped and giggled happily.

"Station!" he exclaimed.

"That's Station?" said Ted dubiously.

"No way," said Bill. "I think there's been some kind of mistake here."

The Grim Reaper rolled his eyes. "You two are so naive," he said. "You just assumed that the most brilliant scientist in the entire universe would be from the little, pathetic planet Earth. You did, didn't you?"

There was some truth in what the Grim Reaper had to say. "Oh. Well. Yeah," said Ted.

But they were getting somewhere. The creatures had stopped jumping up in the air and landing on their heads. They were now aware that Bill and Ted were there, which was something, at least.

"How's it goin', Station-dudes?" said Bill. "I'm Bill S. Preston, Esquire, and this is Ted 'Theodore' Logan and—"

"Station," said the creatures, staring dully at them.

"What are they saying?" Bill whispered to Ted.

"Station," said Ted.

"Station," answered the Stations.

"Yeah," said Bill, "I know what they said, but what does it mean?"

"Maybe they want us to play with them. You know, like gain their trust."

"You mean, jump up and land on our heads?" It was plain that Bill still had his doubts.

"It's either that or leave the princesses to the clutches of Evil Bill and Evil Ted."

"Say no more, dude."

"Station," said the Stations.

It was a pretty easy game, as games went—certainly there were no complicated rules—and it turned out that Bill and Ted were pretty good at it. Given the Grim Reaper's record on games, he didn't join in.

"Station," said the Stations. Bill and Ted joined the two creatures and followed what they did, first running in a circle, then leaping high in the air. At first it wasn't easy getting up enough altitude to make the somersault that allowed for the heavy impact on the cranium. But with perseverance, Bill and Ted—particularly Ted—got the hang of it.

When Ted came in for a particularly good landing on his head, the Stations clapped delightedly, and it seemed as if a perfect friendship had been forged between the two odd-looking creatures and Bill and Ted.

"Way to go, dude," said Bill, "it looks like you won."

Ted jumped to his feet. "That was most jolly. Almost as much fun as breaking rocks in Hell." The Stations crowded around him, clapping vigorously.

They figured it was time to get down to business, and while it was a little strange to explain their problem to two creatures who seemed to have a single-word vocabulary, Bill and Ted figured that the most brilliant scientist in the universe would be able to compensate for this drawback.

"Okay, Stations," said Ted, still elated from his triumph in the landing-flat-on-your-head game, "you have been referred to us as the most brilliant scientist in the universe."

"That is correct," said Bill. "You see, we have a plan and we were wondering if you could give us some help."

"Yah. How would you like to come to Earth and help us build good robot us's and save two beautiful princesses from bad robot us's?" Ted spoke matter-of-factly, as if he were asking the Stations for help changing a flat or blacktopping a driveway or something equally mundane. Of course, the extraordinary was becoming pretty common in Bill and Ted's world—easy travel through time, not to mention guided tours of Heaven and Hell with the Grim Reaper, does tend to make the most bizarre requests sound almost normal.

To their credit, the Stations seemed to take the suggestion seriously—of course, being from another planet, they may have heard this kind

126

of thing every day. After a moment to consider the proposition, they nodded.

"Station," they said.

"Does that mean yes?" Bill wondered allowed. "You know, when you meet a couple of dudes who only know one word, it gets a little, uh, hard to figure out exactly what they mean."

"Station," repeated the Stations.

"Station," said Ted, getting into it.

"Yah," said Bill. "Sounds good . . . Station. You'll enjoy our fair planet Earth. It is a most resplendent place."

Ted glanced at his watch. "Speaking of which, we'd better hurry up. Who knows what those evil robot us's are doing."

The Grim Reaper knew his cue when he heard it. "Let's go . . . dudes."

Death snapped his fingers and everything went black.

The next thing Ted knew someone was tapping on his head. It was not a pleasant sensation, like a love tap, nor was it gentle, like someone trying to get your attention. This was sharp—it hurt—and it was very persistent, as if whoever was doing it was urgently trying to get into Ted's skull in a hurry.

Bill was having a certain amount of trouble with his head too. His hair felt as if someone had woven a few strands of spaghetti into it, and it felt pretty gross.

Bill and Ted opened their eyes at the same

moment and stared around them. They weren't in Heaven or even in Hell anymore. The sun was shining brightly, and wherever they were seemed vaguely familiar. They sat up groggily and looked at each other. As Ted moved, the tapping in his head stopped—in fact, the buzzard that had been pecking at his head flew away, squawking with annoyance at having been cheated of a nice lunch of Ted's brains.

The spaghetti in Bill's hair was a couple of worms who thought he looked inviting.

"Whoaaa . . ." they said, shakily.

"Dude," said Ted, "this is where we died." He looked down at his body and twitched a little to make sure everything still worked. He looked up at the cliff face. "That is truly a most heinous distance to fall."

"Yah," said Bill, "but we're alive."

Bill and Ted smiled at each other and air-guitared weakly.

Ted rubbed his head, fingering the bruises the buzzard had inflicted on his scalp. "That buzzard was totally pecking my head, dude."

Bill pulled the worms out of his hair and flung them away in disgust. "Dinner's over, worm-dude."

"Bill, what happened? Was it a dream? Did we really die? Did we really go to Heaven?"

"Did we beat the Grim Reaper at Twister?" wondered Bill aloud.

"And what about our plan? What about those weird little Station-dudes?"

"Station," said the Stations in their strange little nasal voices. They were standing a few yards away, perched on boulders and staring at Bill and Ted. The two creatures didn't seem to be any worse for wear from their travel from Heaven to the real world.

"It wasn't a dream!" yelled Ted.

"You dudes okay?"

The Stations nodded excitedly. "Station," they said. In this case it seemed to mean that everything was okay.

"But where's Death?"

"Station," they said. This time it meant "heads up" because hurtling down from the sky, his robes flapping around him like wings, was the Grim Reaper. He plummeted to the ground and landed with a heavy thud.

The Grim Reaper lay sprawled in the sand. The Stations thought this was hilarious. They laughed and gibbered and clapped their hands in delight.

"Whoa . . . You okay, dude?"

The Grim Reaper looked bruised and embarrassed, but he was basically in one piece. "Yeah, yeah . . . I'm *just* fine."

Ted helped the Grim One to his feet and dusted him off. "Now what?"

"Okay," said Bill in a take-charge kind of voice. "First on the agenda: get back to town and get cleaned up."

"Second," said Ted, "call the princesses and warn 'em."

"Right, and third: We gotta purchase the stuff we need to make good us's."

"So let's go, dudes," shouted Ted. It certainly was good to be alive again.

The Grim Reaper hobbled after them, muttering to himself and picking leaves and bits of shrub from his hair and clothes. The Stations followed, still giggling at his discomfort. The Grim Reaper turned and glared at them—if looks could kill, you could certainly say that Death's would, right?—and that only seemed to make them laugh even more.

"What's so funny?" demanded the Grim Reaper.

"Station," said the Stations, nearly doubled over with laughter.

The Grim Reaper decided there and then that the next time he reaped someone, they would definitely stay reaped. And he would never play Twister again.

You had to hand it to De Nomolos—when he built the Evil Bill and the Evil Ted, he certainly made exact copies of Good Bill and Good Ted. He could have fixed it that his creations could play the guitar a little better than the originals, but he didn't. Evil Ted was wandering around the Good Bill and the Good Ted's now-totally-trashed apartment, thundering away on Ted's guitar. Awful—really terrible—music wailed, so loud it shook the windows and could have been heard five blocks away.

Evil Bill had to shout to make himself heard on the phone. He was talking to Good Bill's Uncle Milton, a harmless soul who had always stuck up for his nephew. Uncle Milton was shocked at what he was hearing.

"I never liked you, Uncle Milton," said Bill venemously. "You were always, like, a total pain in the neck."

"Bill," said Uncle Milton. "I can't believe my ears."

"Well, believe 'em, dude."

"You know I'm going to have to talk to your father about this."

"Like I care, Uncle Milt. Listen, just flake off, okay?"

Bill slammed down the phone. He shouted over Ted's incredibly loud "music."

"Okay. I totally blew off Good Bill's Uncle Milton. And let me tell you, dude, it was fun. I can't wait to do it again. Who's next?"

Evil Ted stopped "playing" for a moment. The silence was totally golden. "Uh . . . what about that teacher in high school? The dude who was nice to them . . . the History–Social Studies–dude. What's his name?"

Evil Bill snapped his fingers. "Good idea, Evil Ted. Ryan. Mr. Ryan would be totally blown away to hear from us." Evil Bill snatched up the phone and quickly punched in a number.

Mr. Ryan answered on the first ring. "Hello, Mr. Ryan?" said Evil Bill. "Bill S. Preston here."

"How's it going, Bill? I hear you and Ted made it into the Battle of the—"

"You stink, dude," said Bill, cutting him off.

"What? What did you say?"

"You heard me." Bill slammed down the receiver. "That was one surprised dude, dude."

Ted unhooked his guitar and flung it away. It fell with a wild, howling jangle as it slid strings across the floor. "Cool . . . ," observed Ted. "Now, let's do something else totally bad."

"Yah," said Evil Bill. "But like what?" He counted off every evil thing they had done so far. "We killed them already."

"And most resplendently loogied them, don't forget," put in Evil Ted.

"Yah. And we trashed their apartment and messed things up with the princesses. And totally wrecked their relationships with their family and friends. Let's do something else totally heinous."

Evil Ted's eyes lit up. "I know! Let's get them in trouble for insider trading!"

"We don't got the time, dude. De Nomolos wants us to nab the females and get to the concert."

Evil Ted looked very disappointed. "Awww . . . It would be so triumphant."

"Look—I tell you what. We'll take the Porsche and cause trouble on the freeway."

"Like what?"

Evil Bill thought for a moment. "Like driving slow in the fast lane."

"Insider trading would be more fun."

"Gotta improvise, dude."

The Porsche was pretty beat up by now, but it still went fast, so fast that the game of trying to annoy people on the freeway turned out to be no fun at all. With the tape deck cranked up as high as it would go, Evil Bill and Evil Ted wanted to go fast, not slow, no matter how steamed it made the other drivers on the road. They had to content themselves with trying to run over cats on the streets around Missy's house.

Evil Bill was driving and Evil Ted was keeping a sharp lookout for any small creature they could run over. While they had originally thought of cats, anything would do, actually—squirrels, poodles, raccoons—they weren't particular.

Suddenly Ted pointed. "Whoa! There's one, dude!"

"Where?"

"*There!*"

Evil Bill yanked the wheel and the car careened wildly across the street. There was the sound of screaming tires and a cat—it would never know how lucky it was—yowling in the night as it scrambled to get out of the way.

"Just missed!" yelled Evil Bill.

"Dang!" shouted Evil Ted. He immediately looked around for more cats or, failing that, some other way of having fun. But they were running out of time; Missy's house was just up the street. "Dude, we're there!"

"Okay," said Evil Bill. "I have a truly triumphant idea. Take off your seatbelt."

"Why?" asked Evil Ted as he unclipped the harness.

"Because, dude, we're gonna make an entrance!"

"Outstanding!"

Evil Bill steered the car directly at the Logan house, aiming for the picture window in the front of the house—then he slammed on the brakes. The car screeched to a halt, jumped the curb and ploughed onto the lawn. Evil Bill and Evil Ted smashed through the windshield and were headed for the picture window like two circus dudes shot from a cannon, air-guitaring as they went.

In the living room were three very worried young women, each with her own close connection to Bill and Ted—the princesses, Joanna and Elizabeth, and Missy, who at one time had been stepmother to one or the other of the two boys. They were too deep in conversation to notice the sound of the powerful Porsche engine in the street outside.

"We're worried about them," said Joanna. "They are just not the Bill and Ted we know."

"And love," said Elizabeth, softly. "They seem so . . . so completely different."

No one noticed the screech of brakes.

"You know . . . ," said Missy, "I had a strange experience with them myself. It was . . . weird."

"Well, we're not saying that things wouldn't be strange with Bill and Ted."

"Yah," said Elizabeth. "Things do tend to get quite totally strange when Bill and Ted are around."

"But they are never rude. And never inconsiderate."

"Never," agreed Elizabeth.

Just then, Evil Bill and Evil Ted came crashing through the living room window. Glass scattered everywhere and Joanna, Elizabeth and Missy dove for cover.

"Whooooooaaa!" yelled Evil Bill and Evil Ted as they sailed into the room. They crashed to the floor and slid across it, smashing their indestructible metal heads against the fireplace.

Joanna, Missy and Elizabeth peeked out at them, staring, aghast, as Evil Bill and Evil Ted picked themselves up unharmed and dusted themselves off.

"How's it goin', lady humans?" said Evil Bill with a nasty smirk on his face.

Ted kicked a coffee table out of the way, Missy's crystals and tarot cards scattering all over the place. "Hey, Mom, how's about a kiss where it counts?"

Missy jumped to her feet and, unable to restrain herself, slapped Ted hard in the chops. "Don't you speak to me like that! Just wait till your father gets home."

"Whoa . . . am *I* scared."

Evil Bill and Evil Ted each grabbed his respective princess, holding her tight around the waist. The girls tried to pull away.

"Ready for the big night, babes?" said Evil Ted with an unpleasant leer.

"No!" shouted Elizabeth, her pretty blue eyes wide with fear.

"We're not going!" said Joanna.

"Sure you are," said Evil Bill. They started dragging the struggling girls toward the door. Missy blocked their way, putting out both hands to stop them.

"I think you guys better stop right there. We are going to get some things settled right here, right now. Do you hear me?"

Evil Bill and Evil Ted exchanged looks. They may have heard her, but they had no intention of doing anything Missy had in mind.

"Listen," said Evil Bill. "We gotta go." He slugged Missy hard on the chin, knocking her out. "So, catch you later, future wife."

Missy tumbled to the ground. The princesses gasped and stared, first at Missy, then at Evil Bill and Evil Ted.

"Who . . . who are you two?"

Evil Bill and Evil Ted both assumed completely false looks of earnest sincerity.

"Well, you see, girls," said Evil Bill, "it's kind of sort of hard to explain . . ."

"Yah," said Evil Ted. The two exchanged

winks and then unzipped their bodies, revealing that, over their electronic skin, Evil Bill had, in fact, been wearing an Evil Ted suit, and Evil Ted had, in fact, been wearing an Evil Bill suit. That each of them was, in fact, the other, plus the sight of the wires and circuitry that actually formed them—it blinked and clicked like a manic computer—was, to say the least, a little hard on the girls. Joanna and Elizabeth stared wide-eyed and horrified; then, like wilting flowers, they both fainted dead away.

"Whoa . . . ," said Evil Ted, "a brilliantly pointless surprise there, Evil Bill."

"Totally," agreed Evil Bill. "Now, let's bag these babes and take Missy's car."

"On to the Battle of the Bands."

With the princesses slung over their shoulders like sacks, the two robots were about to air-guitar into the night and on to the next and most heinous stage of their evil plan. But just then the phone began to ring.

"Do you think we should answer that?" asked Evil Ted.

"Nawww, what for?"

"Maybe it's someone calling for them, someone we could insult most heinously, further destroying their relationships with their family and friends."

"Good thinking, dude," said Evil Bill. He tossed away his princess as if she were a bag of dirty laundry and raced to answer the phone.

Chapter
9

Good Bill and Ted had managed to find their old van in the desert, where Evil Bill and Evil Ted had left it, and together with the Stations and the Grim Reaper, they went racing into town. The van was pretty much on its last legs, but Bill was pushing the last bit of power out of the old heap. There was one problem: They were going fast, but they weren't sure where they were going at all.

"Where do you buy stuff in San Dimas to make good robot versions of yourself?" Bill wondered aloud.

This was a problem that they had not stopped to consider.

"Hey, Stations," said Ted, "just what kind of,

uh, materials do you dudes need to build these good robot us's?"

The Stations were sitting in the backseat of the van, enjoying the ride as they zoomed down the freeway. They answered Ted's question in the way they knew best. "Station," they said. (What else?)

"I had a feeling they would say that," said Bill.

"What about Radio Shack?" said Ted desperately.

"Closed," said Bill.

"How about Hal's Hobby Haven?"

"That's closed too, isn't it, dude?"

Suddenly Ted had a flash of inspiration. "I know—Builder's Emporium. They always advertise on TV how they never close and have everything the electronics consumer needs."

"Do the ads mention robot building?"

"Well . . . not in so many words . . . But it's worth a shot, right?"

"Absolutely, dude." Bill floored the accelerator, and a few minutes later they were pulling into the brightly lit parking lot of the Builder's Emporium. The thin brakes wailed as Bill stomped on them to bring the van to a halt.

"Okay," explained Bill, "Stations, this is Builder's Emporium, which, we believe, is a repository for all kinds of earthly electronics and robot-building materials. Here you gotta get all the stuff you need to make metal us's. Understand?"

The Stations understood. "Station," they said in unison.

Just as the five of them reached the automatic doors of the giant building warehouse, Ted stopped and sniffed the air. Then he looked suspiciously at the soles of his shoes. "Dude," he said, his nose crinkling in disdain, "what is that most heinous smell?"

Bill sniffed too, pulling open his shirt and sniffing down at his chest. "Ted," he said, "it's us, dude."

Ted took a whiff of the sleeves of his T-shirt, first the left then the right. "It *is* us. How come?"

"We've been dead for hours, dude. It makes you a little, uh, ripe."

"We gotta get cleaned up before we meet the princesses. They would be most grossed out to find that their future husbands smelled like unfresh corpses."

"Totally," agreed Bill.

They were busy washing up in the Builder's Emporium rest room when a big, burly man walked in—he had tattoos on his arms and looked like a trucker—and immediately sniffed the air and frowned. Just because he was a trucker didn't mean he wasn't a sensitive guy.

"Terrible smell," he said.

Bill was scrubbing his face at one of the sinks. "Yah. Sorry."

The man stood in the middle of the room,

not sure if he could take the odor. "Smells like someone died in here. Did someone die in here?"

"Yah," said Ted, "we did."

"*You* did?"

Bill was drying his face now, which was kind of hard to do as the bathroom only had those hot air blowers. "Plus we got a couple of Martians with us."

All this was getting a little weird for the trucker. "You got a couple of whats?"

"Martians," said Ted.

Right on cue, the Stations stepped out of one of the stalls. They nodded pleasantly to the trucker. "Station," they said in greeting.

"Yeah, right," said the trucker, backing toward the door. "You take your time in here, okay?"

"Can't, dude," said Ted, "we've wasted too much time already. "You know where the phones are?"

But the trucker had gone. "Weird dude," observed Bill. "Come on, Stations, we gotta get going."

"Station," said the Stations, nodding.

They fanned out into the store. The Grim Reaper got a shopping cart, and the two Stations hopped up and got in the kiddie-seat— tight squeeze, but they managed—and started down the aisles, which were crammed with all **kinds of household appliances and electronic** gear. The Stations' eyes glittered as they took in all the goods, as if they were little kids let loose in a toy shop.

"Go to it, dudes," said Bill. "Get whatever you need. Me and Ted are going to be over by the phones trying to reach Joanna and Elizabeth."

"Station," said the Station.

"Grim Reaper," said Ted, "keep 'em out of trouble, okay?"

"Yeah, yeah," said the Grim Reaper. He started pushing the shopping cart and discovered that the Stations might be little dudes, but they packed a lot of weight. Huffing and puffing, he steered the cart down the first aisle. The Stations immediately started throwing handfuls of electronic bits and pieces into the cart.

There was no answer at the princesses' apartment. "Where could they be?" said Ted.

"Maybe they went over to our place looking for us. I mean, we've been gone a long time—they must have figured out that something weird is going on, right?"

"Good thinking, dude." Ted dialed his own number and listened as the phone just rang and rang. Finally, he hung up and looked, grim-faced, at Bill. "Nope, they're not there."

"They're not at their place and they're not at ours," said Bill. "Maybe they went to talk to Missy. Why don't you try your dad's number?"

"Good idea," said Ted, hoping that Missy or one of the princesses, not his father, would answer the phone. It would be kind of hard to explain to him where they had been for the last couple of days.

All things considered, though, Ted would have preferred to talk to his father than to the person who actually did answer.

"Logan residence, Evil Bill Preston speaking," said Evil Bill.

"Whoa," said Ted. "Bill, it's the evil you!"

"Bogus," said Good Bill. "What's he doing at your dad's house, dude?"

Evil Bill was kind of surprised to hear from a person he had pushed off a cliff in a desert a long way away and then loogied into the bargain. "Check this out, Evil Ted," he said to his evil partner. "It's them. They're back from the dead."

This didn't seem to faze Evil Ted a bit. "Oh," he said with a shrug. "I guess we get to have all the fun of killing them again."

"Excellent!" said Evil Bill. "You guys are really dead meat this time, dudes."

"No way," insisted Good Ted.

"Yes way," said Evil Bill.

Good Bill snatched the phone out of Ted's hand. "We're gonna get you dudes," he yelled. "This time we're ready for you!" He glanced over his shoulder. The Grim Reaper and the Stations were furiously ripping through the store, their cart piled high with all kinds of stuff suitable for building good robot versions of Bill and Ted.

Good Ted wanted to get in some threats of his own. He grabbed the phone from Bill. "Yah! You dudes don't stand a chance. And where are the princesses? If you two have done anything to Elizabeth and Joanna . . ."

"They're right here, dude," said Evil Bill. "And don't worry about a thing. Nothing's happened to them . . . *yet*." He laughed and slammed down the phone, tearing it off the wall. It fell to the debris-strewn floor in a shower of sparks.

"What did he say?" asked Evil Ted.

"Just that they're gonna be ready for us."

Evil Ted smiled one of his evil smiles. "Well, I think we can be ready for them too."

"Yah. They're never even gonna make it to the concert. We're just too smart for them."

"Totally," said Ted with a little flourish of air guitar. But he stopped mid-note and got a very strange look on his face; his eyes started spinning. It could only mean one thing. A second later and a very angry-looking De Nomolos appeared in his eyes.

"Hail, Evil Genius Leader-dude," said Evil Bill.

De Nomolos was not interested in exchanging pleasantries, particularly not with an electronic moron of his own creation.

"What was that all about?"

"Well, uh, seems they didn't die when we pushed them off the cliff. Sorry."

"Ignoramuses. Both of you."

"Yah. Totally."

"And what did they mean when they said that they were ready for you?"

"Dunno, boss."

De Nomolos snorted derisively. "Begin the emergency plan. You are capable of *that*, aren't you?"

"Totally," said Evil Bill. "Emergency plan. You got it, Great One."

De Nomolos leaned forward and stared hard at them, his eyes seeming to bore into Bill's metal skull. "Do not fail me, you metallic buffoons." Then he vanished from Evil Ted's eyes, leaving behind only a cloud of fuzzy static.

Evil Ted shook his head vigorously, clearing the interference from his vision. "I totally hate it when he does that. No warning, no nothing. And then he totally insults us through my eyes."

"Emergency plan, Evil Ted. You heard the boss-dude."

"Yah," said Evil Ted. "Let's do it."

Evil Bill and Evil Ted pulled up their shirts and reached deep into their electronic guts. Buried deep within them were secret weapons, three canisters full of so much scary stuff that not even Evil Bill and Evil Ted felt comfortable carrying them around. The robots dropped the metal tubes on the floor.

"I'm glad to get rid of these things," said Evil Ted.

"Definitely." Evil Bill shuddered as he looked

at the tubes, which were beginning to split open. Three small creatures—but growing fast—were trying to get out. "Let's go, dude. These things give me the creeps."

They shouldered the princesses and raced out the door, leaving behind them on Ted's dad's living-room floor three growing, breathing horrors.

Bill and Ted followed the Grim Reaper as he pushed his shopping cart across the parking lot toward the van, the Stations toddling along behind them.

"That other me," said Bill, "he's a real jerk."

"Yah," said Ted. "Totally."

Bill pulled open the doors of the van and started tossing in handfuls of the electronic junk they had just bought on instructions from the Stations. It had cost them just about every penny they had left in the world and the last twenty-seven dollars' worth of credit they had on the credit card they had managed to talk the bank into giving them when they first got their straight jobs at Pretzels 'n' Cheese.

Bill looked at the backseat piled high with wires, circuit boards and sheet metal and shook his head. It was not usually in his nature to be pessimistic, but he had never been up against evil robot versions of him and Ted from the future before, and that kind of thing could get to be a little depressing if you thought about it long enough.

"I sure hope the Stations know what they're doing," he said soberly.

"Relax, dude," said Ted. "Don't forget, they come very highly recommended." He glanced at the Stations, but they weren't there anymore. In fact, they were a few hundred yards away, facing each other from opposite ends of the parking lot. It looked a lot like they were about to play their crazy game again—the one that involved landing on your head as hard as you could.

"Station!" yelled Ted.

The Stations ignored him. They didn't even say "Station."

"What are you doing?"

"Dudes!" shouted Bill, "this is not the time to be playing games."

The two Stations had a look on their faces that neither Bill nor Ted had ever seen before. They weren't gibbering and capering or clapping their hands. They weren't even doing the weird little dance that kicked off their game. They looked over at Bill and Ted and the Grim Reaper and nodded at them, calm and confident.

"Station," they said quietly.

"Whoa . . . ," said Ted. "I definitely have the feeling something is about to happen."

"Totally," said Bill.

The Stations started right then. They ran toward each other at a blindingly fast pace, headed right at each other like two hot-rodders playing chicken. They came pounding across the asphalt, their eyes ablaze with a kind of life Bill and Ted hadn't seen in the Stations before. And they weren't running in that flat-footed wobble they had displayed in the past; no, strange though it may sound describing two Martians with big behinds, the Stations actually looked kind of graceful.

At the very last moment, just when it looked as if they would definitely crash into each other, the Stations jumped high, high in the air, like a pair of NBA stars going up for the ball at the tip-off. And then, the Stations sort of high-fived each other, but instead of using their hands, they smacked their bodies together—Thunk!—as hard as they could.

The sound of impact made Bill and Ted wince. The crack of the two Stations smashing into each other sounded as loud and as hard as a shot from a high-caliber rifle.

"Ouch!" yelled Ted.

The very instant the Stations made contact there was a bright flash of light, as if a power-ful electrical circuit had been completed, fol-lowed by a shower of sparks, and then, out of nowhere, out of nothing—literally—except the sheer massive brain power of the two greatest scientists in the history of the universe, came something.

At first, Bill and Ted couldn't quite figure out what it was that had fallen out of the night sky. Tumbling back down to the asphalt of the parking lot was another Station. This one was a lean, stripped-down version of the old Stations, taller, thinner—big butt, but not quite as big—more reserved-looking, more confident. He dusted himself off and walked to where Bill and Ted and the Grim Reaper stood. Of the other Stations there was no sign.

"Station," said the new Station to Bill and Ted. But his voice was firm, commanding, intelligent in a way the old Stations' hadn't been.

"Where'd the other dudes go, dude?" asked Bill.

Ted scanned the night sky. "No sign of them up there," he said.

"Station," said the new Station, pointing to himself.

"Oh. Yah," said Bill. "I get it."

"Get what?"

"Ted, this is the two Stations. When they smacked into each other, they became this dude."

"They *did?*"

"Where else would they go?"

The question plainly was of no interest to Station. He had produced a pad of paper bought at the Builder's Emporium and was busy writing, scribbling at warp speed.

"Now what's he doing?" asked Ted.

"It's like he's writing down instructions on how to make good robot Bill and Teds."

"Yah. We should get hold of that and preserve it for the use of future generations."

"Good thinking, dude," said Bill. "Hey, Station, can we keep that piece of paper?"

"Station!" said Station happily.

Bill took the recipe and looked at it. "Oh, well, never mind." Written on the pad were instructions that only the Stations would ever understand. They read, "Station, station, station, station . . ."

What with the new Station, Bill, Ted, the Grim Reaper and all the stuff they had bought at the Builder's Emporium, the van was getting kind of crowded. The Grim Reaper had crunched into the front seat with Bill, giving the rear of the van over to Station and his valuable work.

The two good robots were lying on the floor with their electronic stomachs open, while Station was working on their wiring like a doctor operating on a patient in a hospital operating theater.

Ted turned in the seat to watch him work. He could hardly believe what he was witnessing. Under Station's sure hands the two robots were beginning to look just like Bill and Ted.

"Whoa . . . ," he said, "way to go, Station. That one's supposed to be me, right?"

Station never took his eyes off his work. He nodded and said, "Station."

Ted examined the other form taking shape. It looked like Bill—in fact, it could have been Bill himself. "Whoa, Bill, you never looked so much like yourself, dude."

"Not bad," said Bill. He took his eyes off the road for a split second to look over his shoulder.

Ted was enthralled at the thought of being present at the creation of another him. He wondered if this was how his father had felt when he was born, but he had a feeling it wasn't.

"How's it goin', Good Robot Me!" he asked.

The voice that answered was lame and kind of metallic sounding.

"*Haaassitdoooin' dooooood.*" Plainly, Station didn't have all the bugs worked out yet.

"You're gonna have to work on that," said Ted.

"Station," said Station in agreement.

"And whatever you do, make sure these robots are programmed to find the babes, wherever they are."

Station nodded. "Station."

"But make sure that the princesses don't like these dudes better than the real us's. That is to say, us."

"Station," said Station.

"That's a relief," said Ted.

Ted wasn't the only one feeling a little insecure. In all the fuss and confusion no one had been paying much attention to the Grim Reaper, and he wasn't used to being ignored. But ever since he had hooked up with Bill and Ted his lot had been nothing but indignity and hard work—melvins, lost games, pushing shopping carts. Now they seemed to be giving him the old cold shoulder on top of everything else. He was beginning to wish he was dead. And he kind of missed the underworld, the old neighborhood as it were.

Ted was still completely mesmerized with the work going on in the back of the van, so the Grim Reaper decided this might be a good moment to find out what was going on.

"Excuse me, Bill," he said diffidently.

"What's up, Grim-dude?"

"Well, I was sort of wondering . . . is there any more I can do for you? I mean, I want to help in any way I can."

Bill shot a worried glance at Death. He was not the tough dude they had met in the desert that terrible morning. In fact, he sounded kind of wimpy. "You, uh . . . uh . . . you can ref, dude. How's that sound?"

It didn't sound good. It sounded to the Grim Reaper as if they were trying to slough him off, get rid of him. Suddenly, he felt like a kid who was the last to be chosen in a baseball game in gym class. The Grim Reaper knew that he had never been popular exactly—he was used to that, it was the kind of thing he expected in his line of work—but he did expect to get a certain amount of respect. He *was* Death, after all.

"Look," said the Grim Reaper, "is there some problem here? I mean . . ." It was hard for him to ask the question. "I mean, what I'm wondering is . . . do you not like me or something? Have I done something to offend you?"

Bill looked over at the very sad Grim Reaper and shook his head as if he couldn't believe what Death was saying to him. "Now, where did you get an idea like that?" He put his hand on the Grim Reaper's bony shoulder. "Death, you're great," he said sincerely. "Me and Ted, we think you're a really nice guy. For real." Bill reached into his pocket and pulled out a pack of gum. "Have some gum, dude."

"No," said the Grim Reaper primly. "I don't care for any, thank you." He turned away, feeling sorry for himself. Death felt like crying.

From the back of the van Ted shouted. "Bill! Check it out!"

Bill craned around for a quick look. The two Good Robot Bill and Teds were far from finished—they were still a rough patchwork, a loosely constructed pair of beings of wire, metal and cloth, as well as some small household appliances, like a blender and a Dust Buster—but they had sat up, jerkily, like a pair of marionettes. They were performing their first attempts at air guitar, which sounded terrible—just like Bill and Ted's attempts on the real thing. The best thing about the two robots was that, like their human prototypes, they had that forever optimistic and friendly look in their eyes, the mark of the real Bill S. Preston, Esquire, and Ted "Theodore" Logan.

"Whoa!" exclaimed Bill. "Not bad!"

"Excellent!" said Ted.

"*Booo-gusss!*" said the robots.

"What?"

The look on the robots' faces had changed dramatically. They were staring fixedly through the windshield of the van. Their bodies jerked spasmodically, and their still unfocused eyes were filled with what appeared to be fear.

"*Booo-gusss!*" One of them managed to get his arm up, and he pointed out at the highway before them.

"What's goin' on, guys?" asked Ted.

All of them stared at the highway. In the middle of the road three figures stood facing them, and behind them was Evil Bill and Evil Ted's Porsche parked across the road, blocking it completely. Bill and Ted couldn't make out the three figures, just their outlines. One was tall, very tall, and shaped like a pear. He had very long, slightly floppy ears. The figure in the middle was small, withered and hunched over and, strangely enough, given that this was the middle of the street, seated in a wheelchair. The last figure was stout, powerfully built and stood hands on hips. There was something very familiar—and scary—about these guys, something that Bill and Ted couldn't quite pinpoint.

Whatever it was, the robots, with their superior brains, had sensed it immediately. They were still in the backseat, trembling with fear.

Bill hit the brakes. "Looks like a roadblock."

"But . . . but that's not the police . . . it's . . . Turn on the brights, dude."

Bill flicked on the high beams, flooding the street with the white light. Bill and Ted screamed the scream of the damned—for their path was blocked by their worst nightmares: Granny S. Preston, Colonel Oats and a seven-foot-high pink Easter Bunny.

Chapter
10

"No waaaaay!" shrieked Bill and Ted, totally unable to believe their eyes.

When it came to scaring people, De Nomolos certainly knew what he was doing. He was a master. In the underworld, Oats, Granny Preston and the Easter Bunny had been horrible enough, but here and now in quiet little old San Dimas they were worse, far worse. Bill and Ted's worst fears, as conjured up by De Nomolos and delivered by his evil robots, were terrifying, and they looked unbeatable, invincible.

Bill and Ted could only stare, horrified, at the terrible apparitions blocking their path. Oats, Granny Preston and the Easter Bunny were no longer just their worst fears; they had been magnified a thousand times over, intensified to the point that they had ceased to be normal human fears and become instead King Kong–sized horrors, terrible monsters that paralyzed them with fear. The three figures before them were Bill and Ted's worst fears on steroids.

Colonel Oats's muscles bulged in his combat fatigues, his face red and frenzied and a mask of fury. He carried a bazooka the size of a length of sewer pipe. Granny S. Preston was scarier-looking than Bill had ever seen her (and he had once caught a glimpse of her early one morning, before she had her face on—the sight had made him shudder for weeks). The stark white hair on her head stood up straight, sort of like the bride of Frankenstein, but not as neat, and the bristly hair on her upper lip and on her chin was as thick and as rough as barbed wire. The Easter Bunny was as tall as Minut Bol but a lot more menacing, mainly because of his teeth, which were big and stainless steel. It looked as if he had a mouth full of garden shears, which was not a feature you normally associated with an Easter Bunny.

"No!" screamed Bill, "it can't be! We left them behind in the underworld."

This was true. Even the Grim Reaper looked puzzled—when he wasn't looking terrified, that is. Scaring Death was something that didn't happen every day.

"No way!" yelped Ted.

Oats stepped forward and pointed the bazooka at them. "Yes way, you pitiful sissies," he snarled. "Now get out of that van. And I mean now. That's an order! And when I give an order, then little worms like you obey it."

Now, Bill and Ted could not be certain of much in their crazy lives, but right then they were absolutely, positively sure of one thing: There was no way on earth they were getting out of that van.

Bill didn't have to think about it; he reacted instinctively. He threw the van into reverse and stood on the accelerator, flooring it. As if the tired old van itself were terrified, a bolt of power surged into the clapped-out engine and the vehicle shot backward. Then Bill cranked the wheel, throwing the van into a perfect 180-degree turn. The bald old tires screamed and smoked as the car whipped in a circle, and inside the van the Grim Reaper, Station and the good robots were thrown around until they were a tangle of arms and legs.

"They're getting away!" stormed Oats. "Let's get 'em."

The Easter Bunny hopped over to the Porsche and bit into the roof, puncturing it as if it were a tin can; then he took his giant, powerful pink paws and tore the whole sheet of metal off. In a matter of seconds the Porsche was a convertible, and it had a seven-foot Easter Bunny in the backseat. Colonel Oats dove into the driver's seat and gunned the engine.

"Throw the old lady a rope," he ordered the Easter Bunny. "Now! You hopping pink stuffed toy."

The Easter Bunny whipped out a rope and tossed it to Granny S. Preston, who caught it neatly.

"Hit it!" she yelled.

"Rolling, you four-and-a-half-foot gray-haired little shriv!" Oats snarled at Granny Preston.

"Drop dead, Oats," Granny Preston snarled right back.

Oats fired up the engine, gave it all the gas he had, all at once, and the powerful car lurched forward, rocketing down the street as if it had been fired from a piece of heavy artillery. Granny Preston, still sitting in her chair, was yanked along behind.

This was certainly not the Granny S. Preston Bill had known his whole life. He was watching their pursuers in the rearview mirror. He gripped the wheel, white-knuckled and more scared than he had ever been before in his life. This just could not be happening to them. No way.

Ted, at the rear of the van, watching through the back window, gulped. "Go faster, dude!" he yelled to Bill.

No matter how scared you might be, no matter how much you might want to get away, it's a simple fact that a twenty-year-old van that has never really run right cannot outrun a new seventy-five-thousand-dollar Porsche. In a matter of seconds, the supercharged black sports car was right on the tail of the van. Ted watched as Colonel Oats yanked the wheel to the right, causing the car to veer and whipping Granny S. Preston to the left. She swung like a tetherball, catching up with the van. She rolled along next to the driver-side window. She leaned in close, her lips all puckered up.

"Hello, Bill," she screeched. "How about that kiss for your little old Granny?" She made these really disgusting little kiss-kiss sounds.

"Yaaaarghgh!" Bill screamed, and he cranked the wheel to the right. The van careened into the other lane, then up onto the shoulder, and totalled a road sign: SAN DIMAS CIVIC AUDITORIUM—ONE MILE. PLEASE DRIVE SAFELY.

Back in the Porsche, Colonel Oats was busy with phase two of his plan. "Get out there," he screamed over the rushing wind and the roar of the engine. "Get out there, you great bouncing, furry egg-delivering behemoth."

The Easter Bunny stood in the backseat and hopped through the torn-up roof, landing on the hood of the car. He paused a moment to get his balance and then hopped again and thumped down hard on the roof of the van, the thin metal buckling under his weight.

The force of the Easter Bunny hitting the roof threw Station and the robots and the Grim

Reaper flat on the floor of the van. Robot Ted smacked his head on the wheel well and his eyes spun crazily.

"*Howwwws it doooooooinnnnn'?*" Robot Ted croaked. He did not look well, what with being only half-finished, rocked and rolled and terrified into the bargain.

"No so good, Robot me," said Ted frankly. "But thanks a lot for asking."

"*Booogussss*," said Robot Ted.

"Station, are they okay?"

"Station," said Station with a shrug. Now Ted really was worried, mainly because he had never seen Station looking worried. Station had that look on his face, like a doctor who thinks he might be about to lose a patient.

"Bill, what are we gonna do? Our robots are getting totally thrashed!"

"I dunno!" yelled Bill.

"Kissy-kissy, Billy," yowled Granny S. Preston, still right there outside the window.

But things were, if you can believe it, about to get worse. Suddenly, two great yellow steel fangs slammed through the roof of the van, slicing through the metal as if it were nothing stronger than aluminum foil. The flashing blades missed the Grim Reaper's head by inches.

The Easter Bunny clawed at the roof and then peeled back the sheet of steel, as if opening a sardine can. He leaned down into the van and glowered at Ted, his hideous face close, as if he were about to bite his head off in a single snap of those murderous teeth.

Spittle dripped from his lips and he leered menacingly, staring into Ted's frightened eyes with fury. "You stole little Deacon's Easter basket."

The words, delivered by an Easter Bunny with murder in his heart, were enough to make any man, Martian, underworld ghoul or robot quail.

Ted and the Grim Reaper screamed. Screaming wasn't yet in Good Robot Bill and Ted's vocabulary, but they expressed themselves the best they could.

"Nooo waaaay! Noooo waaaaay! Noooo waaaay!" they yelled, flailing around on the floor of the careening van.

The amphitheater loomed up ahead of them, so Bill raced the van into the parking lot and slammed on the brakes, laying down yards of smoking rubber. The van came skidding across the lot, shooting like a large, black torpedo straight for a pristine, picture-perfect BMW. The owner of the BMW stared at the van hurtling toward him, and Bill stared back, wondering if his meager insurance would cover the total he was about to inflict on the expensive car. He decided it wouldn't, and at the last possible split second he cranked the wheel, throwing the van into a sideswipe, stopping just short of the BMW.

"Close," said Bill.

Granny S. Preston whirled around the van, roping the doors shut, slamming to a halt right where she had started—just outside Bill's window.

"Hello, Bill," she cooed. "Kissy-kissy for your Granny S. Preston?"

Bill quickly rolled the window shut.

Now things were pretty serious—even Bill and Ted, who, by nature, were inclined to look on the bright side of things, could see that. Their future wives had been kidnapped by evil robots, the Battle of the Bands was about to begin, a homicidal Easter Bunny was trying to claw his way through the roof of their mortally wounded van, and Granny S. Preston had them trapped and was waiting for her kiss—it was hard to see the silver lining in this particular bank of clouds.

"What are we gonna do?" asked Ted in a panicky voice. "We can't shake 'em."

Bill saw that there was only one thing they could do. The very thought filled him with horror. He put a hand on Ted's shoulder. "Ted, there's only one thing we can do . . ." He took a deep breath, steeling himself for what he was about to say. "We gotta face 'em."

Ted gulped. "Bill, you're right. We gotta do it." He looked at the Easter Bunny. "I'll be with you in a moment, dude." He leaned out of the passenger side window and tapped on the glass of the BMW. "Excuse me, dude—I gotta use your car phone. Don't worry—local call."

The BMW driver was still staring, bug-eyed, at the van, and he could be forgiven for not quite believing his eyes. After all, it wasn't every day you came across a van besieged by an elderly woman in a wheelchair, not to mention saw a giant Easter Bunny attempting to devour any kind of vehicle.

Stunned, he passed the phone through the window. "Sure," he said in a faraway sort of voice. "Help yourself. Take your time. No hurry."

" 'Preciate it," said Ted.

Bill was ready to face the music. He took one last look at Granny S. Preston and slowly rolled down the window. He looked like a man headed inexorably for the gallows . . .

Ted dialed his home number, and when his little brother, Deacon, answered, he spoke in a rush, a great torrent of words.

"Hello, Deacon, it's Ted. Listen, dude, ten years ago at Nana and Pop-pop's house, I totally stole your Easter basket and ate all your candy."

Deacon knew his brother Ted to be a slightly, well, *unusual* person, so this sudden confession of a petty theft committed some ten years before didn't startle him all that much.

"You did, huh?" said Deacon.

"Yes, me," said Ted, his voice full of contrition. "I did it. I did it and I'm sorry."

"Fine," said Deacon. "Now we know who pulled off the crime of the century." He hung up, wondering how it was that he and Ted were related. It just didn't seem possible sometimes.

The instant Ted confessed his crime, the Easter Bunny stopped moving, stopped clawing at the roof of the van.

Bill had placed his lips against Granny S. Preston's leathery, hairy skin and, with superhuman effort, managed to give her a little smack on the cheek. Then his grandmother got a very sweet look on her face—she wasn't really a heinous old lady, just a little scary if you had to kiss her regularly—and patted Bill on the knee.

"Now," she said in that old lady voice of hers, "that wasn't so bad, was it, Billy?"

"No, Granny S. Preston," said Bill dutifully, as a good grandson should.

The Easter Bunny was gone, replaced by the evil-looking tube from whence he came. It rolled off the roof and fell to the asphalt of the parking lot, shattering into a million pieces. A split second later, Granny S. Preston turned into her own cylinder and dropped, it too shattering the minute it hit the ground.

Bill and Ted heaved huge, deep sighs of relief. The Grim Reaper, Station and the Good Robots couldn't be quite so restrained.

"Station!" screamed Station.

"EEEEEXXXCCCEEELLLEEENNNTTT!" yelled Good Robot Bill and Ted.

But they weren't out of the woods yet. In their euphoria, they had forgotten that there remained one powerful, determined enemy, meaner and tougher than the Easter Bunny and Granny S. Preston combined—Colonel Oats. Bill's spirits plunged and fear coursed through him when he saw, in the rearview mirror, the Porsche screech to a halt and Colonel Oats emerge toting that big bazooka of his. He walked slowly toward the van like a bad guy in a western. The guy was definitely trouble.

"Uh . . . Ted," said Bill.

Ted followed the line of Bill's worried gaze. "Uh-oh . . ."

Colonel Oats did not look happy. He hated being let down by an Easter Bunny and an old lady—they would not have been his first choice of allies. "Useless hippity-hoppin' pain in the neck," he muttered, loading his artillery piece. "Stinkin' no-good rolling little shriv. I'm gonna have to do this all by myself." He slammed a shell into the chamber and cocked the weapon.

Bill and Ted looked at each other and gulped. The Easter Bunny and Granny S. Preston were pussycats compared to an angry creature from the underworld carrying a large-caliber weapon.

"How are we gonna get rid of him?" yelled Ted.

"Dude," said Bill, "there is only one way to get rid of a guy like this."

"There *is*?"

"Yah. We gotta use the one weapon that we have that he has no defense against."

"We *do*? What?"

"We gotta kill him . . ."

"Totally," agreed Ted.

"Kill him with kindness, dude."

"Oh. Yah. Right. Kindness."

"Okay," said Bill authoritatively. "Everybody—Death, Station, Robot Us's—we gotta be totally nice to this dude, got it?"

"But," protested the Grim Reaper, "he has a gun. A very large gun."

"Ignore it," advised Ted.

"Okay," said Bill. "Everyone look friendly." Bill pushed open the sliding door of the van, while the rest of them organized themselves into a nice little conversational group and did their best to smile at the man pointing a bazooka at them.

Colonel Oats looked down the long barrel, sighting the weapon squarely on Ted. "Decided to give up, huh?" he barked. "Better this way. Puts you outta your misery."

Ted smiled pleasantly. "Colonel Oats, this is a pleasant surprise. Great to see you. Come in, dude."

"Huh?" said Colonel Oats. "Why aren't you scared? I like to see the fear in their eyes before I waste my victims."

"Scared?" said Ted with a laugh. "Why would we be scared of you, Colonel Oats?" Bill and the rest tittered politely, as if they were well-mannered guests at a sedate little tea party, astonished that anyone would think that *they* would be scared of a gentle soul like Colonel Oats.

"Yah," said Bill. "We couldn't be scared of an old teddy bear like you, Colonel."

"It's like you're a member of the family," added Ted. He was rooting around in the glove compartment of the van and had come up with a small, rather worn selection of junk food. He held out a cake wrapped in cellophane as if trying to feed a skittish animal. "Twinkie?" he asked.

"Family . . . ?" said Colonel Oats, his voice quavering. "And a Twinkie?"

"Or perhaps our guest would prefer a Ding Dong," said Bill "or a Snow Ball."

The Colonel Oats from Hell felt a strange, warm and not altogether unpleasant sensation creep over him. It was the uncommon feeling of having someone like him, of having someone be kind to him. He let go of his heavy weapon, and the bazooka clattered to the ground.

"There," said Ted soothingly, "that's better, isn't it?"

"Come on in, pal," said Bill, "have a seat, have a Ding Dong and unburden your soul to us."

"Your friends," added Ted.

"Friends?" said Colonel Oats, his jaw quivering. He allowed himself to be drawn into the van and settled on one of the seats.

"Eat, Colonel Oats," said Bill. "You must be terribly hungry. It's been a long day."

"Yes . . . ," said Oats wearily. He heaved a tremendous sigh and brushed a hand through his sweaty, matted hair. "I'm so tired."

"There, there," said Ted.

"Yah. Relax. You're among friends, dude."

"Friends," said Colonel Oats, dreamily, as if the word were part of a magic incantation.

"Friends," reiterated Ted.

Colonel Oats looked from one friendly face to the next and felt a lump rise in his throat. He took a large bite from the Ding Dong, spilling crumbs down his chin and onto his battle fatigues. It tasted wonderful.

"I . . . I . . . I wasn't always like this . . . ," he said sadly. He looked like a man with the weight of the world on his shoulders. "I wasn't always a bad person."

"You," said Bill, "bad?"

"Pshaw," said Ted.

Suddenly, Colonel Oats found that he was seized by an overwhelming desire to confess, to unburden his soul as Bill had suggested he do.

"You see, when I was a teenager—scarcely more than a little boy, really—my father used to spank me . . . he used to spank me with an ammo clip. He . . . he frightened me." Suddenly the hurt and fear of those days, feelings so long suppressed, came flooding back into Colonel Oats's tortured psyche. His eyes filled with tears and his voice shook. "Now I realize that what I have been doing for the past twenty years was just an attempt to be the kind of boy Daddy wanted me to be . . ."

"Sadistic," suggested Bill helpfully.

"Twisted," said Ted.

Colonel Oats nodded sadly. Robot Bill stroked his hair and Robot Ted patted him gently on the shoulder. Even the Grim Reaper looked touched. He, of all people, knew what it was like not to be liked.

Colonel Oats didn't realize it, but, like the Easter Bunny and Granny S. Preston, he was losing his effectiveness, under the influence of the unrelenting kindness of Bill and Ted and his other newfound friends.

"What I've been doing for the past twenty years is terrorizing young people—all to please my daddy."

Ted nodded. "That's an important epiphany, Colonel Oats."

"Yah," said Bill. "But you don't have to do that anymore now do you?"

"No," said Colonel Oats in a very small voice.

"Promise?" said Ted.

"Yes," said Colonel Oats.

"Good," said Bill. "Catch you later, dude."

And, in that instant, Colonel Oats transformed back into one of the evil tubes and shattered.

"Well," said the Grim Reaper. "I'm sure glad *that's* over."

Chapter
11

San Dimas may not have been the entertainment capital of the world, but things were pretty exciting that Saturday night. News of the Battle of the Bands and the recording contract that would go to the victors had spread through the San Dimas garage band subculture, and the fans were out in force to cheer on their champions. Kids who had been grounded, or who couldn't get tickets, were watching the concert on the live TV feed. All eyes were on the San Dimas Civic Auditorium.

The interior of the arena was packed, the fans standing in the aisles or on their seats, the real metal experts down front, crushing up against the stage, deafened by the music that thundered out of the towering stacks of amplifiers. These were the real fans and a tough crowd to please: If they liked your act, then they went wild. If they didn't, then you knew all about it.

Backstage was crowded with band members. Those who had just come off looked elated or crestfallen, depending on the reaction of the crowd. Those who were just about to go on looked nervous—for most of the bands in the competition the San Dimas Civic Auditorium was a great step up venue-wise. Few of them had played anything bigger than the back room of a bar, a private party—maybe a high school dance or two. Never anything this big or anything with rewards even remotely as great. No wonder they were nervous. Of course, they had never dealt with Hell, the Grim Reaper, evil robots or murderous Easter Bunnies, so, when put in perspective, the San Dimas Battle of the Bands was not all that big a deal.

Mrs. Wardroe was like a general commanding an army. She stood backstage with a clipboard in her hands trying to keep track of who was who and who went on when. A band was just finishing up its set when she realized that Wyld Stallyns was on next. The auditorium was still jammed—she had been sure that most of the crowd would have gone home by now—so her plan for putting Bill and Ted on late in hopes that they wouldn't embarrass themselves—and her—too badly in front of too many people seemed to have backfired.

She was too harried and too exhausted by

her long night's work to notice that Bill and Ted seemed different from the last time she met them. They were lolling backstage, cocky sneers on their faces, their instruments slung casually around their necks. They were acting as if they didn't have a care in the world. Of course, she had no way of knowing that she wasn't dealing with the real Bill and Ted, but with Evil Bill and Evil Ted. She was just relieved they had shown up.

The band on stage finished their last number with a dissonant crash of chords and a wild thundering of drums, a finale that had always sounded pretty good to them, in a garage, that is, but tonight sounded kind of pathetic. At least it sounded kind of lame to the audience, which responded with only lukewarm applause.

"Okay," said Wardroe to Evil Bill and Evil Ted, "you guys ready? You're up."

"We're ready, babe," said Evil Bill.

"Yah. Totally."

"Wait a minute," said Wardroe. "Where are the girls?"

"Hanging around," said Evil Bill.

Evil Ted looked up into the forest of scaffolding and girders suspended over the stage and holding the lights and more amplifiers. "We just tied 'em to the rafters," he said, with a chuckle.

"Em-hm," said Mrs Wardroe, studying her clipboard and not really listening. She was completely worn out from the long hours she had put in to bring this show to the stage, but if she had bothered to look up directly above the stage, she would have seen Joanna and Elizabeth—both scared to death—trussed tightly in the rafters.

"Yah," said Evil Bill, "we're gonna totally kill 'em as a finale."

"Em-hm," said Mrs Wardroe. She had so much on her mind she just couldn't pay attention to everything the "talent" talked about. "Well . . ." She glanced out at the stage; the band there was just finishing up. They hadn't gone over too hot. And with Wyld Stallyns bringing the show to a close, it looked like the San Dimas Battle of the Bands was definitely going to end not with a bang but a whimper. "Well, all I can say is good luck, gentlemen."

"Station," said Evil Bill.

Good Bill, Good Ted, the Grim Reaper and Station clustered around the Good Bill and Ted robots.

"Well," said Ted, "this is it."

"Okay, robots," said Bill, like a coach prepping his team before the big game, "you know what you have to do."

"*Saaave the baaabes*," said the good robots.

"That's right. Station, think they'll be able to pull it off?"

Station did his best to look confident. "Station," he said.

"Yeah, I figured you might say that," said Ted.

"Good luck," said Bill.

"Yah," said Ted. "Totally."

"Go get 'em!" yelled Bill, like a starter beginning a pair of runners in a fast forty.

And then the robots were off, shooting away like bullets. They took off incredibly fast, so fast that their long, awkward metallic strides left fiery footprints smoking and glowing behind them in the parking lot asphalt. They took off so fast, in fact, that it took a second or two for Bill and Ted to realize that the robots had made a terrible mistake. Truly the bugs had not been worked out of their systems.

The robots had taken off in the wrong direction, running *away* from the auditorium instead of toward it. In a flash they were gone—too late for Bill and Ted to stop them.

"Hey!" shouted Bill. "Wait!"

"Where are you going?" yelled Ted.

But the good robots were covering so much ground so fast that they were out of earshot almost instantly. Bill and Ted stared, dumbstruck, through the billowing smoke the good robots left in their wake.

"Back to the drawing board," said Ted, sadly.

"Station! What's going on dude?"

But Station had changed too. The calm, confident Station, the one who had built the malfunctioning robots, was gone, replaced with his old two selves. But they seemed different too—they were drained of energy, as if the effort of building the robots had been too much for them.

"Look," said Ted, "they are totally wiped out."

"Station," croaked the Stations dully, nodding in agreement. Then they turned and, mustering what little energy they had left, pitter-pattered away, following in the footsteps of their good robot creations.

Bill, Ted and the Grim Reaper stared after them. It seemed as if the plan was not going to work, that all the trouble and terror they had been through had been worth nothing.

"Now what do we do?" asked Ted.

"We still gotta stop them."

"Yah. But how? I mean, it was going to be hard enough to stop two evil robot dudes who had already killed us once even if we had help from good robots. But now . . ."

"Well, we still gotta try."

Ted's jaw set in a determined line. "You're right, Bill. It's the least we can do."

They took off at a run for the auditorium, the Grim Reaper huffing and puffing along behind them. The backstage entrance was marked, Artists Only.

"Artists," said Bill, "I like that."

The security guard on the door didn't even bother to check their names on the master list of performers—all he had to do was take one look **at the Grim Reaper, dressed as he was, to know** that he had a heavy metal band on his hands.

The Grim Reaper might have gotten them in, but he was slowing them down. He was a lot older than Bill and Ted—by about thirty thousand years—so he wasn't as fast on his feet as he could be. By the time he got backstage, he was sweating profusely and completely out of breath.

"Come on, dude!" yelled Ted.

"Hurry," urged Bill.

"I'm coming, I'm coming," panted the Grim Reaper. "Give a guy a break."

"Death," said Bill urgently, "you gotta help us stall for time."

"Yah. We gotta check things out. Find the princesses. Make a plan."

All this totally flustered the Grim Reaper—which puzzled Bill and Ted, as you would have thought that a guy in his line of work would be used to improvising in unusual situations. They dragged him toward the wings. The sound of the crowd was much louder now, a low roar like the breaking of surf on a beach.

"How?" stammered the Grim Reaper. "I don't understand . . . I'm not really prepared for . . . I mean, I haven't worked up anything to say . . . I haven't got a thing to wear . . ."

"This is important, dude," said Ted seriously.

"You *gotta* cover for us while we try and figure out what to do. It's a matter of life and, well, death."

Ted took the Grim Reaper by his shoulders and looked into his bloodshot old eyes. "Death. We need your help. In the van I heard you telling Bill that you wanted to help us—well, here's your big chance, dude."

"But . . . I am frightened," said the Grim Reaper unhappily. "All these people . . . you know how I work, fellas. I'm a lot better one on one."

Bill and Ted couldn't waste any more time convincing the Grim Reaper. They shoved him out on to the stage. "You're going out there Death . . ."

"And you're coming back a star," said Ted.

They shoved the Grim Reaper into the glare of the lights and left him to do his best.

Mrs. Wardroe was doing her thing at the microphone, ushering out the band that had just finished and preparing her introduction of Evil Bill and Evil Ted.

"Let's give a big hand to the last band, Primus, weren't they great?" Actually, Mrs. Wardroe and the crowd knew that Primus wasn't all that great, but she had to say something encouraging—it was only polite. There was a spattering of applause from the audience, not exactly a ringing endorsement. But Mrs. Wardroe couldn't help thinking that if Wyld Stallyns got as good a response, Bill and Ted would be very, very lucky.

"And now for our final act of the evening . . .

Please give a warm welcome to Wyld Stallyns!"

Evil Bill and Evil Ted strode onto the stage, their guitars slung over their shoulders like weapons. Both evil robots wore nasty little smirks, so delighted were they with the thought of the havoc they were about to wreak on Bill, Ted, the princesses, the Battle of the Bands and on history itself. It was a great day to be in the business of doing total evil.

The crowd clapped, but not with a lot of enthusiasm. If the Wyld Stallyns had achieved any measure of fame in San Dimas, it was as the worst garage band going, bar none. Some of the audience groaned when they heard the band name, others started toward the exits.

Evil Bill stepped up to the microphone and looked with disgust at the entire audience. "How's it goin', worms?" His amplified voice boomed through the auditorium. "I am Bill S. Preston, Esquire."

Evil Ted leaned into his mike. "And I am Ted 'Theodore' Logan. And we are . . ."

"Wyld Stallyns!"

"We know!" shouted one of the spectators down front right by the stage.

"Don't remind us," yelled someone nearby.

Evil Bill and Evil Ted ignored this heckling—hurt feelings were not part of their programming. Evil Bill shouted:

"And we're hear to say . . ."

"All hail, Mr. De Nomolos," Evil Bill and Evil Ted yelled in unison. They swung their guitars up and flailed wildly at the strings. The manic thrashing at their instruments failed to demonstrate that Bill and Ted had improved in the music department. Mrs. Wardroe covered her eyes with her hands. More and more people started up the aisles towards the exits. It looked like the Wyld Stallyns set was over before it had begun.

Then, strangely enough, the Wyld Stallyns' act took a sudden turn for the better. The Grim Reaper tottered onto the stage, staring at the crowd, smiling nervously. "Hi . . . ," he said with a wimpy little wave. Then, overcome with fear, he fainted and smacked his head on the synthesizer keyboard. A musical vamp started out of the machine. The crowd that remained was curious now. It wasn't every band that managed to get a guest appearance by the Grim Reaper, even if it was a brief one.

Then Evil Bill and Evil Ted caught sight of the real Bill and Ted entering from the wings. The evil robots stopped banging away at their guitars and stared. Somehow—and it did seem kind of improbable—Bill and Ted had managed to outwit Colonel Oats, the Easter Bunny and Granny S. Preston—and that was the most evil De Nomolos knew how to conjure up. No wonder Evil Bill and Evil Ted were surprised.

Suddenly, the auditorium was very quiet. The crowd was intrigued—maybe the Wyld Stallyns really sucked musically, but there was something to be said for their showmanship. After all, two sets of identical musicians plus the prostrate figure of Death on the stage were out of the ordinary.

"It can't be," said Evil Bill into his open microphone.

"No way," said Evil Ted.

"Yes way," insisted Good Ted.

"You totally killed us, you evil metal jerks," said Good Bill.

His words drew a measure of applause from the members of the audience who appreciated a little psychodrama with their music. Everyone seemed to be holding his or her breath, wondering what was going to happen next.

Evil Bill and Evil Ted had recovered from their shock and surprise and were beginning to realize that they were going to have the fun of killing Good Bill and Good Ted all over again plus the charge of doing away with their girlfriends at the same time. This would truly be a night that San Dimas would not forget in a long time.

"We killed you," said Evil Bill with a sneer, "and we're gonna do it again."

"Yah!" said Evil Ted, "*and* we're going to kill your girlfriends!"

Evil Ted pulled a long knife out of his belt and sliced through a thick rope tethered just offstage. The princesses dropped from the catwalk above the stage, plummeting toward the hard floor. Joanna and Elizabeth screamed, but **just as it looked as if they were going to smash** to the ground, the ropes jerked them back and they hung suspended over the stage.

The crowd roared its approval of this truly excellent display of showmanship. Maybe the Wyld Stallyns *had* improved. Even Mrs. Wardroe looked mildly impressed.

But to Good Bill and Good Ted, this wasn't a show, this was real life. Seeing their girlfriends treated so roughly was more than they could stand. With outraged screams, the two charged across the stage.

"Joanna!" yelled Good Bill.

"Elizabeth!" shouted Good Ted.

"We'll save you, babes!" said Good Bill.

"Yah! Hang on!" said Good Ted. Good advice, but under the circumstances, there was little else the princesses could do.

But Evil Bill and Evil Ted had other plans for Good Ted and Good Bill. The robots fell on our heroes, grabbed them and tossed them into the back wall of the stage as if they were about as heavy as pillows.

Boom! Bill and Ted smacked into the hard bricks and slid to the floor, stars dancing in front of their eyes. They shook their heads like boxers trying to clear their brains after a savage right, but even in their befuddled state, Bill and Ted realized that they were not off to a good start. De Nomolos may have created these robots in their image, but he had made a little improvement—like superior strength.

The crowd, however, was eating it up. Other

acts in the Battle of the Bands may have played better music, but no one put on a show like this. Applause filled the auditorium to the rafters.

The Grim Reaper heard the clapping and the cheering and awoke from his daze. He saw his friends lying sprawled at the base of the wall, and he took in Evil Bill and Evil Ted's look of total triumph and figured he had to act, no matter how scared he was of appearing before big crowds. He mustered all the confidence he had and stepped up to an open microphone. Even before he opened his mouth, the Grim Reaper got a big hand and that made him feel better.

"Hello, San Dimas!" he said, his deep voice booming out through the auditorium. The crowd roared back. But they weren't quite sure where they should be looking. On the one hand you had a dude dressed—very convincingly—as Death at the mike, on the other you had two dudes beating up on two dudes who looked just like them. Evil Bill and Evil Ted were advancing on Bill and Ted, coming in for the kill, cornering them against the back wall of the stage.

"Got you!" snarled Evil Bill, in triumph.

"Prepare to die. Again!"

"You good-for-nothing, lesser-developed human prototype versions of us!"

"Guys . . . ," said Ted weakly. "Let's talk."

The Grim Reaper was totally getting into the acclaim he was getting from the crowd. He started snapping his long, thin fingers and immediately improvised:

"I am Death. I come from beyond. I reap each soul with my bony wand . . ."

Evil Bill and Evil Ted had gotten hold of Bill and Ted now and, with a cruel, inhuman surge of brute force, threw our hapless heroes across the stage, body-slamming them to the ground as if they were wrestlers—but this was for real. The crowd was screaming now. This was a show! There was a triumphant fight going on, a rapping Grim Reaper, not to mention two truly resplendent babes suspended over the stage.

The Grim Reaper was steadily gaining in confidence.

"Behold before you, two Bills and two Teds. These two good and real . . ." He pointed to the Good Bill and the Good Ted sprawled on the stage. "These two, true metal heads. And so my good friends—Oomphf!" Evil Ted pushed the Grim Reaper away from the microphone, sending Death flying.

"Shut up!" he ordered. "I need this." Evil Ted grabbed the mike stand and tossed the microphone away. Holding it as if it were a club, he stalked toward Good Bill and Good Ted. Evil Bill got the same idea, grabbed a heavy microphone stand and started toward his own victim.

Seeing this development, Good Bill and Good Ted were, as usual, in total agreement. "Bogus," they moaned.

No one seemed to be paying much attention

to the princesses, but they were in as mortal danger as Bill and Ted. The ropes that bound their hands were beginning to fray, and they were just seconds away from plummeting to the floor of the stage.

"Bill, I think we are about to be dead. Again."

"Heinous."

"Totally!"

"We gotta think, dude."

"Dude, I can't think of anything right now except for maybe death."

Death, it seemed, was thinking of his new-found career in show business. He moon-walked—badly, but he was new to the business—across the stage and took his place in front of another open microphone.

"Tonight you will witness their ultimate battle. The winner will rightly mount the Wyld Stallyns saddle."

Okay, so it didn't rhyme exactly, but it was close enough and the crowd was eating it up.

Bill had been thinking, and he wasn't much better at it than Ted. "Ted . . . there's only one thing to do."

Saved, thought Ted. "What?"

Evil Ted and Evil Bill were standing over them now, their microphone stands raised high over their heads.

"Don't move," said Bill.

"*What!* That's it? Don't move?"

Evil Bill and Evil Ted swung, and the heavy mike stands caught Good Bill and Good Ted square in the temples. Their eyes turned up in their heads and for a second everything was black.

"We got 'em," said Evil Bill.

"Totally. Finally."

Indeed, it did look as if this were the end of Bill and Ted. Their bodies were sprawled lifeless on the stage, not moving a muscle. The crowd was real impressed, and even Mrs. Wardroe thought that the boys were doing an excellent job of acting.

The crowd was cheering wildly, stamping their feet and demanding more. Evil Bill and Evil Ted faced their adoring public, drinking in the acclaim like champagne.

After a second or two, the spirits of Bill and Ted, looking just as they had the first time they died, rose out of their corpses and looked down at the bodies that had once been their mortal forms.

Ted did not look impressed. "That was your idea?" he asked in disgust. "Stand still? We're dead again, dude."

"Ted. How many games did we beat the Grim Reaper at?"

It seemed like a long time ago. "I dunno, four I guess—why?"

"And how many lives did we use to get back here?" asked Bill, as if patiently explaining an algebra problem to a student.

"Uh . . . two." The full import of Bill's plan suddenly sunk into Ted's brain. His eyes widened in delight. "Whoa! Yah! The Grim Reaper still owes us two lives!" He cupped his hands around his mouth and called over to the Grim Reaper, shouting to make himself heard above the thunderous applause. "Hey, Death, you still owe us two lives, don't you, dude?"

The Grim Reaper, though, was enjoying his moment in the spotlight, so into his own performance that he was oblivious to Bill and Ted's predicament.

"Yo! Death!" shouted Bill and Ted.

The Grim Reaper glared at them. "Can't you see that I am performing?"

"But, dude . . ."

The Grim Reaper hated being annoyed, but he knew he had to honor his promise. "Yes," he shouted over his shoulder. "You can come back."

Bill and Ted jumped for joy and did a ghostly high five.

"Let's get 'em, Ted!"

"Go for it, Bill!"

They dove back into their bodies and leaped to their feet.

Evil Bill and Evil Ted were facing the audience, unaware that Good Bill and Good Ted had come back to life and were out for revenge.

"Remember the name," Evil Bill was screaming at the crowd. "Mr. Nomolos de Nomolos!"

"The Greatest Man in History!" shrieked Evil Ted.

The two evil robots turned to each other and

high-fived. "We've totally won, dude!"

But they hadn't. Good Bill and Good Ted came up behind them, grabbed the evil ones by the ears and yanked, pulling the robot heads from the robot bodies.

"No waaaay!" yelled the heads.

"Yes way, Evil Bill and Ted heads!" responded Good Bill and Good Ted.

Without their powerful bodies, the robots were much easier to deal with. The headless bodies staggered around the stage wondering where their heads were. "Over here!" yelled Evil Bill's head, but as the bodies approached, Bill and Ted struck out at them, kicking the flailing, hapless figures off the stage and into the audience.

Ted cocked his fist and punched the Evil Ted robot head hard and square in the jaw. "Take that!" Pow! He slammed him again. "And that!" Cracking him in the nose.

Bill readied his furious fist. "Got any last words, malevolent pate?"

Evil Bill's eyes flicked toward the rafters. "Yah! Check out your girlfriends!"

Bill looked up. "What? Oh no!"

The ropes that bound the princesses' wrists had just about frayed through. In that instant, the strands gave way, Joanna and Elizabeth dropping in a sickening fall toward the stage and certain death. All Bill and Ted could do was watch helplessly.

Then, suddenly, the back wall of the stage

shattered in a shower of bricks and Good Robot Bill and Ted crashed through, running straight under the falling princesses, their metallic arms out as if they were wide receivers going out to catch a long, long, bomb.

"*SAAAAVE THE BAAABES! SAAAVE THE BAAABES! SAAAVE THE BAAABES!*" they intoned.

And save the babes, they did. The robots judged the falling princesses perfectly and so— boom-boom—each landed right on target in the robots' outstretched arms.

"Whooooaaaaa!" said Bill and Ted in relief and admiration. "Excellent!"

The Stations were not far behind the robots, and they were now climbing through the hole smashed by Good Robot Bill and Good Robot Ted. The crowd was delirious now—there were two decapitated Bill and Teds, plus two kind of strange Bill and Teds, *plus* a set of normal Bill and Teds in this show. Never mind the Grim Reaper and what appeared to be a pair of Martians.

Bill clapped the Stations on the shoulders. "They *did* know what they were doing!"

"Yah!" shouted Ted. "And they must have had to run around the whole world to get up enough momentum to burst through that wall."

Bill and Ted, the evil robot heads tucked under their arms, extended their free hands to the princesses.

"Ladies . . ."

Joanna and Elizabeth curtsied and took their fiancés' hands, and together they stepped to the front of the stage to receive the applause and adulation of the crowd.

But then: the whole auditorium seemed to tremble, followed by a loud howl and a flash of blinding blue-white light. Suddenly, crashing down onto the stage, came a time-traveling phone booth. It landed in a shower of crackling, sizzling electricity. The door slid open and there, robed in black, stood De Nomolos. He did not look happy, but he managed a thin little smile when he caught sight of Bill and Ted.

"William S. Preston, Esquire?"

"Yah," said Bill.

"And Ted 'Theodore' Logan?"

"How's it goin', Circuits of Time—travel-in'—dude?"

The crowd had gone very quiet all of a sudden, as if they were now witnesses to a scene of great drama. They all knew that whoever the dude in the phone booth was, he was a dude to be reckoned with.

"Shut up," snapped De Nomolos.

"Who are you?" demanded Ted.

"Who am I?" The question seemed to amuse De Nomolos. In the future it would be a very silly question indeed. "I am Nomolos de Nomolos." He pointed to the evil robot heads. "I am the master of those morons. And I must see to it that you die."

Bill and Ted looked at each other.

"Die, dude," said Bill, wearily.

"Again. Don't you dudes ever think of anything else, except trying to totally kill us?"

"No," said De Nomolos truthfully. He swept aside his robe and pulled out a huge twenty-fifth-century–style handgun.

"Okay," said Ted. "You've been trying to kill us for days now. Maybe you'd like to tell us why."

"Yah," said Bill. "Why, dude?"

"It is very simple," said De Nomolos. "So that in my day—seven hundred years from now—I will rule. All I need do is kill you and return to the future. When I arrive, I will be revered, an emperor. A living god!"

"Oh," said Bill.

"Got you," said Ted.

"And now," said De Nomolos, "it is time . . ." He cocked the huge weapon and aimed it straight out ahead of him, like a dueler. He decided to kill Bill first, alphabetical order.

"Now what?" Ted whispered. "Now we got no lives left."

Bill was fresh out of ideas. All he could do was shrug.

"Gentlemen," shouted Mrs. Wardroe from the wings, "*use your heads!*" She pointed to the robot heads still tucked under their arms. Evil Bill and Evil Ted were watching De Nomolos, and they were grinning expectantly.

De Nomolos fired twice, the big gun roaring and bucking in his hand. Bill and Ted thrust the robot heads up, blocking the blast, the bullets ricocheting around the stage like hornets. Then they cocked their arms back and rolled the heads toward De Nomolos, as if they were champion bowlers throwing perfect strikes.

De Nomolos gaped at the heads rolling toward him, the self-destruct buttons built into the robot crania having been activated by the force of the gun blast.

The evil genius could only smile feebly, weakly, as certain destruction rolled toward him. "Guys . . . I was only joking . . ."

The two heads hit his legs and stopped. There was a blinding flash and a sizzling *zzzzzaaaaapppppp* followed by three sheets of blue flame, and when that was gone, De Nomolos and the evil robot heads were gone. In their place were three piles of smoking ash.

The crowd had never seen special effects like this before. They were cheering, whistling, stamping their feet. The applause was deafening. To tell the truth, Bill and Ted had never seen anything like it before either.

"Dude," said Ted, awestruck, "where'd they go?"

"I dunno, dude."

The Grim Reaper brushed and buffed his fingernails and tried to look modest. "Really, guys," he said, "I'm surprised you had to ask."

"They've been reaped?"

"Totally," said the Grim Reaper.

Bill pointed to the floor. "So you'll be seeing

them later . . . down there."

"Yup," said Death.

"Well, let me give you a piece of advice, dude," said Ted. "Don't play Battleship with them. It's not your game."

"Don't worry," said Death.

"So who was that guy?" asked Bill.

Mrs. Wardroe walked out onto the stage. "Perhaps I can answer that question for you, gentlemen."

"Mrs. Wardroe . . ." said Bill.

"Thanks for the help," said Ted.

"Yah, we definitely—"

"Whooooaaaa!" said Bill and Ted. "Another one!"

Mrs. Wardroe was doing an Evil Bill and Evil Ted, totally tearing apart her body, but instead of yet another enemy emerging, a very friendly and welcome figure appeared. Mrs. Wardroe's face disappeared, and in her place was Rufus, cool Rufus, Bill and Ted's mentor and guide in all things having to do with time travel.

"Rufus!" yelled Bill and Ted.

"Rufus!" yelled the princesses.

"*Ruuuufusssss!*" said Good Robot Bill and Good Robot Ted.

"Station!" said you-know-who.

"How long have you been here, dude?" asked Bill excitedly.

"I got here just in time for your audition, William."

"So you were Mrs. Wardroe all along?"

"That's right."

"Then who's this?" asked Ted, mystified.

Rufus pointed to the pile of dust that had once been De Nomolos. "That, amigos, was Mr. De Nomolos . . . my old gym teacher and the sit-up champ of the twenty-seventh century. A man whose ideals were so incongruous with the times that he had to force others to share his world view . . . but, fortunately, thanks to you, he has failed."

Bill looked at the pile of smoking ash and shook his head. "A most ignoble ending, Mr. De Nomolos."

"But we're glad you came to it," said Ted.

"And now, gentlemen, the stage is yours." Rufus gestured toward the microphones and the crowd.

Bill and Ted gulped. "Thanks, dude . . ."

The Wyld Stallyns were a much bigger band now. Rufus picked up a guitar, Joanna crossed to the keyboards, Elizabeth to drums. The Reaper took a stand-up bass, the Stations on percussion. Even the good robots got in on the act, trying to clap along. They were pretty lame, but their electronic hearts were in the right place.

Bill and Ted looked into the crowd. It was the same old problem. Time travel, evil robots, Easter Bunnies with murder in their hearts, Heaven, Hell, the Grim Reaper—piece of cake. Talking to the crowd, playing their instruments—no way.

"Bill . . . what are we going to say?"

"I dunno. But it better be good."

All eyes were on them, the crowd figuring that a little music shouldn't be too hard for dudes like Bill and Ted to arrange. After all, they had gone to a lot of trouble with the rest of the show. The guys looked at each other for a moment, their brows furrowed. Then Bill looked over at the Grim Reaper and got an idea. Once he had been scared of Death. Now they were pals. There was a moral in that—if only he could find it.

He stepped up to his microphone. "Kiss your fears, dudes," he blurted out.

"Yah, or just call 'em," said Ted, picking up the thread of Bill's thought. "Call 'em up and offer 'em a honey bun or something. And maybe they'll get smaller, and maybe even go away."

"Yah," agreed Bill, thinking of Granny S. Preston. "They're not that bad."

"Here's what's bad: evil robot versions of you."

"Yah," said Bill. "Never allow yourself to get programmed by anybody other than yourself." Bill glanced over his shoulder at the Stations and the good robots. "Unless maybe a Martian."

The Stations clapped happily. "Station!"

"Beyond that," said Ted, "all we can say is . . ."

"Let's play!" yelled Bill and Ted together.

The crowd roared as Bill and Ted launched into their first number. It was a good thing the crowd was making so much noise, because otherwise they would have heard how terribly the band was playing.

Bill and Ted could tell, though, and they were disappointed. They were going to lose their fans almost before they had them.

"Dude. After everything that's happened, we still don't know how to play."

Bill nodded sadly. "Maybe we oughta get good, Ted."

"How?"

Both of them looked over to De Nomolos's phone booth and had the same thought at the same time. A little time travel never hurt.

"Joanna!" yelled Ted. "Elizabeth! Get in the booth!"

Bill turned to the microphone. "Ladies and gentlemen, excuse us a second." Then he too stepped into the booth and disappeared, leaving the crowd staring in disbelief.

The audience, not being really hip to time travel, didn't have too long to wait, not even time to get disappointed, because a matter of seconds after the phone booth vanished in a cloud of sparks it reappeared, blasting back onto the stage.

Everything happened so fast that it seemed at first as if nothing had changed—as if nothing *could* change in a matter of seconds—but as soon as the door of the booth opened, it was obvious that there had been some major changes in the leaders of Wyld Stallyns.

For one thing, Bill and Ted looked older—not a lot older, but enough to make an impression, say about a year and a half—because in the few seconds they had been gone, they had actually traveled sixteen months in the Circuits of Time, going back in time so they could *really* prepare for this very important gig.

They were dressed completely different. Gone were the denims and sweats, replaced by professional black leather costumes designed and sewn by Elizabeth and Joanna. Their hair was different too—Bill wore a long beard and Ted had grown an impressive mustache. Although inside they were still the same old Bill and Ted, externally they didn't look like Bill and Ted, they looked like rock stars. And they played like rock stars too.

"That was a fast sixteen months of intensive guitar training," Bill whispered to Ted.

"Yah, except for that two-week honeymoon we spent in Medieval England with the princesses."

"Time well spent, dude." Perhaps the biggest change in Bill and Ted was what they had strapped to their backs. They stepped up to the mike and turned, revealing to the crowd the two little babies they had on their backs, carried in little baby backpacks.

"Hello, San Dimas," said Bill. "Say hello to little Ted!"

"And this is little Bill," yelled Ted.

The crowd screamed welcome to two new

members of rock's aristocracy. The proud mothers, Joanna and Elizabeth, stood in the background beaming.

"One, two—one-two-three-four!" Bill and Ted counted off and then launched into amazing, over-the-top, indescribably masterful guitar solos. The music blazed out over the crowd, loud melodic fire that seemed to grip the audience and lift them up high to the heavens. Wyld Stallyns had arrived. They had fulfilled their destiny.

Rufus only had one thing to say to that: "Station."

Things hadn't quite worked out the way De Nomolos expected them to. In fact, things couldn't have been worse. But the dude deserved it.

A split second after Bill and Ted zapped him and the evil robots, all three of them found themselves in the underworld.

It was bad enough being dead, De Nomolos thought, but he hadn't figured on having company, particularly Evil Bill and Evil Ted. All his plans in ruins, he was dead and now this.

"What are you doing here?" he snarled at the two robots.

"How's it going, Mr. De Nomolos?" said Evil Bill spritely.

"We're your worst fears, Mr. De Nomolos," said Evil Ted, "and I guess you're going to have to get used to us, dude."

"I am? Why?"

" 'Cause you're going to have to spend all eternity with them," said the Grim Reaper, looming over him.

"Death," said De Nomolos, "just the man I want to see. How about a game, a nice friendly game of Battleship? Twister? Clue?"

Death smiled and shook his head slowly. "No way, dude, no way."